I0571267

The Reflections of Queen Snow White

By

David Meredith

Text copyright © 2017 David Meredith
All Rights Reserved

Acknowledgements
To anyone who has ever known loss, wrestled with grief, and struggled to find themselves again.

*

Special thanks to Matt Hughes for his beautiful artwork on the cover of this novel. You can discover many more of his exceptional pieces at:

www.MattHughesArt.com

"Then the king's son, full of joy, said, 'You are with me... I love you more than everything in the world. Come with me... You shall be my wife.' Snow White was willing, and went with him. Their wedding was held with great show and splendor and they lived together happily ever after..."

The Brothers Grimm – Tale #53

Reflections

Real things so long past they are no longer real

Elsewise

Forgotten in a steady stream of years which washed away that
effervescent creature of an antecedent age
Like the portrait of a stranger

Eyes of long abjured youth stare back

Certainly you could have never really been that person

Too full of light and mirth and potency of spirit – naivety

Innocence betrayed – defiled.

Opaline dreams now wraithlike and dim.

Nothing left but the waiting now and the

Silentious solitude of everlasting repose

TABLE OF CONTENTS

Chapter 1

With a shrill keen the two young hawks soared over snow-capped peaks, reveling in the newly come spring. The day was crisp and clear and even the dullest of their race would have been able to see for dozens and dozens of miles in every direction. The world spread out beneath them in helpless submission and their proud shadows ghosted across the vastness of their dominion; first over the rocky crags, then the greening slopes of the cool, grassy foothills and finally the muddy fields of the fertile bottom lands, which would soon be tilled and planted anew with wheat, hops, and barley. Together they wheeled and dove and swooped then climbed once more to do it again, rapturously sailing a sea of air a thousand feet above the dwellings of mortal men.

Lord and Lady of the sky they were, their majestic cries echoing through the clouds as they flew. Magnificent they had been separately, flying high and solitary against the azure sky, hunting for prey with sharp eyes unblinking and then with exultant cries, plummeting to Earth like deadly meteors. Together however, they were something more, so much more.

The aerial dance of the two lordly birds was joyous, triumphant. It exhibited an effervescence of being that could only come from the supreme contentment they found in doing just exactly what nature had wilt them. It would have been regarded as a beauty and a marvel, by anyone able to see it.

Sadly however, no one did.

It was not because it was a secret thing. In fact, the two mighty raptors vaunted their greatness all over the sky! They announced their approach with resonating shrieks that echoed through the upland hillocks and hummocks grandly proclaiming; "Here we are! Gaze upon our majesty if you dare!" But the mortals below were simply too distracted by the hum drum comings and goings of their own mundane existence to notice. Had they but lifted their eyes just a little, their very souls would have been uplifted.

Still, the lack of an audience did not diminish their performance. Their swooping flight was not for show. The two mighty hawks whirled and soared to edify themselves. Their peerless dance was for each other and ever would be, for when a hawk takes a mate, it is for life.

On this magnificent day, high above the world, witnessed only by the sun, the clouds, and the cerulean sky they celebrated the consummation of their union. Today they had begun the lofty reel that they would continue all of the days of their life together. Together they would face the hazards and travails of these harsh lands. Together they would protect the vast territory they claimed just as they would also guard their young and each other. Together, just like today, whenever the chance might come, they would thrill again to the simple joy that they found in each other's company as they cavorted high above the land, wild and free.

From their lofty perspective in their revelrous marriage dance they could see, though they certainly did not understand what it was, preparations for a wedding ceremony that would be, if perhaps not quite as vigorous as their own, competing with them for magnificence. Below them sat a great fortress of men, which had been built long ago, high upon a jagged cliff. It was accessible only from one side through the single tall gate that breached the towering walls. Its spiring towers stretched skyward as if yearning for the heights that were so comfortable to the feathery king and his lady. Each minaret was hung with banners and flowers, white silks and ribbons. Every inch had been scrubbed to a brilliant sheen in anticipation of the joyous celebration to come.

The grounds were a hive of activity. Frantic workers and gaily clad nobles rushed this way and that on their urgent ways and a great multitude of artisans and merchants streamed in and out of the gate like a never-ending work line of ants. Every inch of the castle seemed busy and eager. Every corner seemed to resonate with laughter and fair speech… Except, perhaps, for one.

Had Lord and Lady Hawk been able or even inclined to gain entry into the one quiet, cavernous room in question, they might have wondered at the contrast. They might have asked; what in the world could be so impervious to the joyousness all around? Then again, perhaps they unlike any other would have understood the dysphoria all too well, shivered with dread, and then gone back to their marriage nest to banish the bleakness with the comfort of each other's warm, feathery bodies.

In a word, the chamber was vast. In fact, the ceiling soared nearly high enough to build a proper aerie in the rafters - but it was also vastly empty. It seemed strangely bereft of the blithesome decorations bursting like wild spring blossoms from every other nook and cranny around the palace.

The cavernous chamber appeared a bleak island of melancholy set adrift upon a sunny, celebratory sea. The sunlight shining through high vaulted windows was wan and sickly. The air felt stagnant and stale and an inexplicable aura of weighty despair seemed to permeate everyone and everything within.

There were only a few very subdued people in the throne room. A scant half-dozen soldiers or so stood about the walls at regular intervals all correctly straight and diligent, liveried in pristine white, but even that immaculacy felt muted somehow. They may have well as been nothing more than disused and superfluous furniture, long forgotten and attracting little notice or concern. Rather, one's attention was drawn instead to an improbable duo situated in the center of the room.

One was a small, slight figure who threatened to disappear upon a massive, intricately carved wooden throne, which was displayed proudly on a high, raised dais. The other, standing at the base of the tall platform, was even tinier and more curious still. His droning, monotone voice was the only sound, echoing hollowly across the otherwise silent chamber.

"...Have already received gifts from the nearest lords," he said. " It is quite a selection I must say - honestly a bit excessive if you want my opinion on the matter - but still not nearly all of it yet. I expect that the gentry from further out will simply bring theirs with them the day of the wedding, which as you know creates infinitely more work for me, but I shall endure and catalog everything received so that her Majesty may send appropriate reply in a timely manner. I do think that in particular you should make a special effort to thank Duke Gewissenhoft. The carriage he sent for the honeymoon is quite exquisite to say nothing of the horses..."

Queen Snow White was not really listening. Her mind was wandering again. She seemed to get lost in her own thoughts so easily these days! The distant cry of some far-off bird of prey startled her and she sat up abruptly on her throne.

The years had been kind to her. Her ivory skin was still supple and mostly unlined but for the tiniest hint of crow's feet around her eyes and the thinnest of creases at the corners of her mouth. Her coal black hair was shot through with silver now, but rather than make her look elderly it simply made her seem regal. The thin circlet that Charming had set upon her brow the day of their marriage so long ago was clipped firmly in place and her long hair hung flowingly about her shoulders. The dress she wore was simple green silk but of the highest quality available and her artfully painted, brown eyes were sharp and keen.

At least, they generally were. Right now they looked a bit glazed over. She rubbed at them restlessly and realized that she had only partially heard what her diminutive steward was saying. She must have dozed off.

That, of course, was easy enough to do when being briefed by the impeccably dressed and dapper, if incredibly long-winded, little old man. The queen dearly loved him and he had been her stanch friend and indispensable advisor for many years now, but honestly! Did he have to go on so?

The wizened little counselor was reading off an extensive list of new arrivals who would be guesting at her castle for the wedding celebration and the gifts received thereof, paying careful note to those which he felt were the most deserving of a direct display of gratitude from her royal self. Even now, during what was supposed to be a patently joyous occasion, the gentry were still jostling and jockeying for her favor and that of young Princess Raven. Every gift received was more lavish than the one before as each of her nobles tried to outdo his or her fellows, hoping for some smallest crumb of royal regard to fall their way. Snow White found it to be positively exhausting.

She suddenly realized that she had totally failed to hear what the little man in front of her had just said. He was looking up at her expectantly.

"I'm sorry, Erfreut," the queen apologized with a small, self-depreciating smile. "I'm afraid my mind was wandering... What was that last bit?"

"I *said* your daughter has also requested an audience with you, Majesty. I think her feelings have been hurt by your... unavailability of late. She has submitted a formal request through the Judicial Ministry."

"She did what?!" exclaimed Snow White sitting forward abruptly. "Why on Earth would she do that? She knows she can always just come to me..."

The little man shot his queen an almost disrespectfully dubious glance and cleared his throat officiously. "If I might note,

4

Highness, the young princess has attempted to seek your presence nearly a dozen times this week alone and has always found her mother... indisposed. If I might make so bold, I think her a bit... shall we say... frazzled. Wedding jitters perhaps, but in any case..." The elderly dwarf quickly changed the subject and barreled on with his exhaustive docket of concerns.

"Shall I put Lord Stolz in the Green Room?" He asked. "He is certainly deserving of the honor given his rank and long service to your husband, but I already have Count Bemessen in the Red Room next door, and you know how *they* are. Those two never get along and I would like to avoid dueling in the corridors if I can help it, but I also worry that if we put Lord Stolz further away he will feel slighted, and that would be at least as bad. What do you think?"

"I think I'm tired," stated the queen wearily with a grimace. She put her head in her hands.

Maybe the little man before her was not the problem. It felt like another one of *those* days. There had been far too many of them lately. She fell positively morose and did not want to deal with anyone or anything, particularly not petty political bickering among her nobles. Snow White sighed; slumping down in the extravagantly decorated, but patently uncomfortable chair and rubbed her temples. The queen glanced at the even larger, empty chair to her left. Charming had always taken care of this sort of thing. *He* had been the political one.

Her eyes abruptly grew moist and her lower lip quivered. The idea of his strong, even voice not echoing through this great hall still seemed inconceivable. Over her entire reign, the queen had rarely come here without him. In fact, she so connected his comforting presence with this room that even now, she kept turning to his vacant seat to offer some comment or ask for his advice ever forgetting that he was not there. Nor would he ever be. It felt so wrong, so... *unnatural*.

Snow White stared at the empty chair. She shook her head, chiding herself sternly. It *had* been over a year after all. He had been quite a bit older than her, and they had both known that this time would most likely come. They had even talked about it before - Often in fact, as they lay wrapped in the comforting warmth of each other's arms in the enormous canopied bed that they shared for over thirty years, staring into the darkness late at night after a long session of... She sobbed loudly. Why did it then still hurt so much?

The Queen looked away from Erfreut to hide her tears. Maybe it was because back then it had always been talk of 'what if' and 'someday'. The reality of his passing had proven far more difficult than anything she had ever even imagined before. She felt so alone, so positively *abandoned*.

Her steward did not fail to notice his queen's distress. He ordered the guards to leave and in less than a second was at her side. Erfreut took her tiny white hand gently in his own rough, brown paw. The mantle of councilor fell from his voice and posture like a discarded cloak might have fallen from his shoulders.

"What is it, Snowy?" The elderly little dwarf asked gently. His calloused fingers stroked hers softly. "This should be a happy time. Prince Edel's a wonderful man. Raven loves him... Couldn't hope for better'n that..."

"Oh, I know, Erfreut." Snow White sobbed shaking her head helplessly. "I just miss him. Charming should *be* here for this. It's just not right. We were supposed to live happily ever after! I suppose we did for a very long time, but... It's just not fair, Erfreut! He should be here. That's all..."

"Aye, my girl." Erfreut had cultivated his courtly speech since coming to Castle Wolfejager, but that was not really him. He spoke now in the familiar brogue he used when first they had met so long ago. In the blink of an eye he had transformed from royal steward to lifelong friend.

"Aye, he should be, lass." He went on gently. "Ain't fair at all, for him to miss this day comin'... Givin' his girl away and all... But I've gotta say... It ain't fair for *you* to miss it either. Do try to buck up, if not for yourself then for Raven at least..."

When they had first met so long ago, he was the youngest of the then princess' seven forest companions. They were so kind to offer up shelter and companionship to a bedraggled young woman who had shown up so unexpectedly on their doorstep, and the queen had never forgotten it. They too were all gone now - all of them but Erfreut that is. Snow White had been horrified at the thought of the little old man living in the forest in that big lonely cottage all by himself and so had invited him to come to the palace to work.

Erfreut had proven surprisingly adept at politics however, and rose swiftly through the bureaucracy until he became the royal family's most trusted advisor. Ever since Charming died, he had seen expertly to the day to day running of the household and management of the various ministries. Now the tottering steward was indispensable to the bereaved queen. Snow White had no idea what she would have done without him, nor did she really want to reflect on the possibility too deeply.

"'Tis alright, Snowy," he continued soothingly. His eyes shone with sympathy. "There be no shame in tears. God knows I shed enough for me boyos when they passed one right after the other until I was all who was left. I know what you feel lass - a big empty spot right here."

He left off stroking her porcelain hand to thump his chest.

"It's where the little piece of your heart used to be that ye shared with them. You don't ever get that back, but the pain dulls in time and ye start thinking back to all the good things ye used to share together... That, My Dear One," he smiled at her kindly. "That is when you realize that they aren't gone all together - That they did leave little pieces of themselves with you. That's when you can really cherish it.

"You still miss them, o' course," he continued. "Oh! What I wouldn't give to have a good night o' drinking with me boyos again and some good loud singin' too, I tell ye! But, you find the strength to go on and even to be happy again..." He paused and sighed sadly. "What I wouldn't give to see ye smile again, lass. I mean *really* smile with joy in your heart like ye used to. Bright as the sun it was...."

"Thank you, Erfreut." The queen squeezed his larger scabrous hands with both of her tiny soft ones. She met his eyes sincerely. "You keep me going. Do you know that? I don't know what I would do without you. I'd be all alone if not for you."

She sighed in frustration and released him. "I just can't seem to see any light anymore! Everything seems so dark and gray and hopeless. I want to be happy again. I want to share in my daughter's joy at her wedding, but it just feels like a huge part of my soul is missing.

"I feel like a wraith!" She complained. "Half here, half gone... I just don't know how to be happy anymore. Every time I start... Every time I'm doing something that *ought* to be fun, that *should* be amusing, that I *used* to enjoy, I just can't help feeling it isn't half as good as it would have been if Charming were here with me."

"Well do I know that feeling, lass, but don't you worry, Snowy. It'll come. It'll come." He patted her hand reassuringly once more before descending the dais. He seemed suddenly to stand straighter. His voice went back to the indolent tones of royal steward. "Now, if her Highness finds herself a bit indisposed I might perhaps ask her leave to see to the additional preparations in her absence?"

The change back into the snooty timbre of the Court came so abruptly that it appeared her friend had transformed into a completely different person right before her eyes. It was a necessary masquerade though, and Snow White smiled in spite of herself at how expertly the tiny oldster donned the required mask of his position.

"Thanks Erfreut," She sighed gratefully.

These arrangements had to be made and the queen knew it, but Snow White just did not feel up to coping with them right now. Her mood was too black, too melancholy to plan any sort of joyous celebration.

"As always, I trust your judgment. I think some time alone would do me good..."

Erfreut frowned. "Now I don't know about that, Highness. Perhaps I could organize a luncheon, or a picnic? Maybe a minstrel would make you feel..."

"Thank you Erfreut, but no." The queen interrupted kindly but firmly. "I simply wish to be alone right now. Perhaps tomorrow..." She let the half-finished sentence trail off into silence.

Erfreut sighed. "Indeed, Majesty." The elderly dwarf bowed low to his queen. When he spoke he did not sound very optimistic. "Perhaps tomorrow... I shall go and see to today's wedding arrangements and inform you when they are completed."

He bowed then hobbled his way toward the exit of the huge audience chamber. The little man rapped twice upon the enormous doors leading in, which immediately swung open under the labors of two grunting guardsmen. Then he quietly departed. The doors quickly clanged shut behind him leaving Queen Snow White alone in the cavernous throne room. It was nearly as empty as she felt right now.

Snow White had said she wanted to be alone, but that was not really true. She simply *was* alone, whether there were any other people about to witness it or not. Now that she was by herself in the large room however, the queen was not at all sure what to do next. This of course was her regular dilemma. It seemed difficult to do anything anymore but sit around feeling miserable and sad. She sighed dejectedly and decided to make her way to her private chambers.

Perhaps, she thought, *a bit of a nap would do me some good.*

However, as soon as she entered her apartments and dismissed her ladies-in-waiting, Snow White knew she would find no rest here. The candles were all extinguished and the grate was tightly shut above the cold, dark hearth. Sunlight shone in through an open window, but not directly. It illuminated the chamber with a dim, half-light. The huge four-poster bed in the far corner seemed clothed in shadow. It did not look the least bit comforting. Rather it felt lonely and sinister. The idea of it made her start crying again.

This had always been her sanctuary. She had always cherished this space for its warmth and serenity. It was perhaps the only place in the whole world free from the prying eyes of ambitious courtiers and salacious gossips - where she and her husband could truly be at ease and unguarded with each other. Neither enmity nor ill will had ever been allowed to cross the threshold of this chamber, she mused. It had always been a place of love and comfort before, but now it just seemed cold and empty and... She felt lost in here, she realized.

Snow White stared at the bed for a very long while. It was still familiar, but changed; no longer welcoming and safe. It had become strange to her somehow – as if all the life had drained out of it with the death of the king. It seemed to reflect the horrible emptiness within her that so often felt like it wanted to swallow her up from the inside. She leaned her head against the bed post, closed her eyes, and again began weeping. This was not how she was supposed to feel! Not here.

The queen abruptly realized she had no desire whatsoever for a nap. She did not want to be anywhere near that large, lonely bed. She quickly retreated.

This will never do! She thought critically, furiously rubbing at her eyes. *Look at me! Going to pieces over a silly piece of furniture...*

The queen took a deep, calming breath. She just needed to get her mind on something else. She needed a diversion.

Snow White briefly considered taking a stroll around the gardens. It was springtime after all. The sky was cloudless and blue today and the flowers were all in bloom. The veritable legion of gardeners who cared for the grounds had been hard at work ensuring that the royal arboretum would be especially resplendent for the upcoming nuptials. The bright sunshine, beautiful flowers, and fresh spring air could hardly fail to improve her mood, could they?

Then the queen thought of the hundreds of nobles currently guesting at her palace for Raven's wedding. The gardens were bound to be *infested* with them and she certainly did not feel up to all of the petty political posturing and obsequiousness that even a simple stroll among such company would entail. Especially with her frayed emotions, she did not have the patience for it today.

Still at a loss for what to do, she at length decided to simply walk around her shadowy palace until she thought of something more substantive. Snow White purposefully chose halls and corridors that she knew would be empty. The few servants she passed bowed respectfully as the queen strode by, but quickly scurried off to complete whatever chores or errands they had been assigned. She wandered aimlessly. Anyplace she might choose to go seemed equally pointless to her at the moment, but Snow White also decided that moving somewhere was preferable to sitting still with only her self-sorrowful musings to keep her company.

Twice she almost came upon a party of nobles, boisterously trooping down the hall from the opposite direction in the full gay spirit of the upcoming festivities. These, the queen scrupulously avoided - the first by quickly turning down a handy adjoining hallway and the second by ducking into a conveniently darkened door. She grimaced in distaste until she could no longer hear the clamor of them any longer.

Snow White had no desire whatsoever to converse with the likes of them at all today if she could help it. She preferred solitude to mixing with that bunch, but that particular attitude was not a product of her grief. She remembered all too well that for all of their pretty clothes and correctly courteous manners, there was not a one of them who was anybody to be trusted. Most of them, she knew, would turn on her in a heartbeat if they thought it was to their advantage and that they could get away with it. Snow White had learned that particularly hard lesson all too well.

As the last of the second group of noisy party-primped and gaily clad high-born paraded out of earshot, Snow White grimaced again, but also took a moment to collect herself and get her bearings. This was not a part of the castle that she frequented. It was honestly one that she had consciously avoided almost the entire time she had lived here with her husband and king. The narrow doorway she had randomly stepped into did not lead to a room or closet, but rather to a long and winding set of stairs. Snow White was unsure if she had come this way purely by accident or through some unconscious pull of her own melancholy, but now that she realized where she was, she had very little desire to stay.

Still, it *was* quiet here. This entire wing of her massive palace had only been used for storage now creeping up on nearly thirty five years, as long as she and Charming had lived here together in fact, and there was very little chance of anyone coming to disturb her. As much as the place unnerved her, Snow White realized that she was unlikely to encounter anything more unsettling than dust or rats. So ultimately, she closed the stubborn door to the main corridor behind her and began the steep climb up the long tower stairs.

Chapter 2

It had been many years indeed since Snow White last ascended these stairs. It was almost a lifetime ago in fact, and she marveled at the unkind changes that time and disuse had wrought. The rusty iron torch brackets on the wall were empty and dark, the only evidence of their ever having been filled at all the faint black soot marks upon the wall behind them and the ceiling above. The only light illuminating the narrow staircase now was what little sunlight leaked in through the irregularly spaced and boarded up windows along the climb. It was enough to see by, but gave the winding stair an air of the sinister, as if something dark and menacing lurked ahead just out of view.

The dust that blanketed everything was thick and undisturbed. She left not only the obvious track of passage made by the train of her gown upon the stairs, but also delicate handprints on the visibly deteriorated railing, now only loosely bolted to the dingy walls. The queen doubted very seriously that it would hold her weight if she happened to miss a step. Idly she thought that the climb was bound to ruin her dress and that she really ought to get back to more wholesome surroundings, but she did not slow her footsteps. Her need for solitude too was great.

With her breath more than a bit labored, she finally reached the top. As she raised her head, a single heavy oaken door came starkly into view. Snow White froze. Despite the long years that stretched in between, she felt a little of the old dread as she approached the doorway to Lady Arglist's chambers. Her predecessor had also sought the solitude of this lonely tower.

She recoiled at the thought and almost retreated back down the stairs the way she had come, but chided herself immediately. There was nothing to fear. Nothing and no one lay beyond this moldering portal to torment her any longer. It was just a door and beyond that just an empty room.

They had never gotten along well. Snow White understood from very early in her relationship with her stepmother that the other woman wanted no part of her at all. It was clear that even in the beginning, she saw Snow White as nothing but unwelcomed competition for King Garion's affections.

At first it was simple disinterest, but after her stepmother failed to become pregnant, Lady Arglist viewed Snow White with a bitter, jealous resentment. Then when Snow White reached about eleven years of age, her father the king became ill and died unexpectedly of a fever. That then put Arglist in the unenviable position of acting as regent to the child of another woman, in an unfriendly court, where she was poised to be replaced and rendered totally irrelevant as soon as that child came of age. Without Snow White's father to keep it in check, that initial acrimony had festered and warped into naked, unadulterated hatred.

Though it shamed her, the dread Snow White felt in her childhood returned almost as forcefully now as she put her hand on the hard wooden door. The queen stared at the door. She found her heart was beating very swiftly and a cold sweat broke out on her palms and at her brow.

It's just a door... She reminded herself firmly. *Yes, just a door and beyond that just a room.* Her tormentor, who had once dwelt within, was long dead. The former regent queen could no longer hurt her.

As if to belie that thought, the landing where she stood suddenly became darker. She knew that it was most likely as simple as a cloud passing briefly before the obscured sun outside, but still the increased dimness filled her with foreboding.

It is just a room! She thought to herself sternly. *Charming saved me from all of that! It's long since over and done!* But still she hesitated.

Maybe Charming was her problem now, she thought sadly. She had become so accustomed to her handsome prince rushing swiftly to her side whenever she was in need, that she found she hardly knew how to deal with anything anymore. His comforting presence had given her confidence to make decisions she never would have dared and do things that she feared were far beyond her.

Perhaps it was because he had always believed in her, or maybe it was because somewhere deep in the back of her mind she could tell herself that her husband could fix anything that went really poorly...

Snow White grimaced at the idea. It made her sound pathetic, even in her own mind. She scowled at herself in irritation.

No silly door is not going to defeat me! She resolutely determined. *I am queen!*

Snow White marshaled her strength, took a deep breath, growled low in her throat, and pulled. The heavy door grated slowly into motion with a loud groan of protest.

A sudden flurry of grey accompanied by a horrible squawking racket made her jump nearly out of her skin, and Snow White shrank back into the stairwell. Though her pounding heart felt like it had jumped nearly into her throat, she managed a chuckle at her own foolishness - just a roosting flock of pigeons. She had startled them and they had taken flight - nothing more. She entered Arglist's chambers.

The long disused apartments were gently lit by the early afternoon sun. Visible beams of sunlight streamed in through several large unshuttered windows illuminating billions of floating dust moats to beautiful effect. A warm spring breeze gently whipped and swirled around the chamber in a way that would have been pleasant if it did not also stir up decades of choking dust.

The chamber showed obvious signs of the birds' long time residence. Although all of the furniture had been covered with canvas sheets, everything bore the stains of years, successive nestings, and generations of bird droppings. These ominous furniture ghosts were then stacked all around with unwanted boxes upon boxes of odds and ends that had not been discarded from other places about the castle. These too bore signs of the birds' habitation, many torn into by tiny claws and contents strewn or serving as the housing for nests.

One old nest that was immediately within Snow White's view had obviously been at least partially constructed from frayed bits of silk out of the former regent-queen's wardrobe. Another contained bits of garishly pink dyed wicker that may once have been a little woven box or spring hat. A dead rat skeleton lay in one corner, and a partially uncovered loveseat that had nearly all of the stuffing ripped out of it and scattered about the room sat in another. The ceiling was heavily draped with dingy cobwebs.

In the midst of all of this disarray Snow White mentally contrasted the now with what had been. The large canopied bed in which Arglist had slept was pushed squarely against the wall opposite where it was when the former queen dwelt here. The numerous wardrobes, dressers, and chests that contained the vain queen's innumerable garments and gowns had been hastily shoved all together in one corner of the room. Most of the other fine furnishings the former regent had used were piled unceremoniously against a third wall. In fact, *nothing* was as it had been before, Snow White thought.

Then something caught her eye - A silvery glint beneath an enormous tarpaulin, revealed as the corners of the rough fabric whipped and flapped in the brisk spring breeze. It jogged her memory.

She strode across the chamber, grasped the great canvas sheet with both hands, and swept it aside. When she beheld what was beneath, she caught her breath and amended her previous thought. Nothing was as it had been but for this - a massive, full-length, gilded mirror. It towered over her reaching from floor to ceiling. It must have been nearly fifteen feet tall.

This she remembered. It had been precious to Arglist. Snow White recalled the slender woman standing before the huge looking glass turning this way and that in whatever new outfit she had just bought for herself - primping and preening, thoroughly entranced by her own elegance and beauty.

Arglist had talked to the mirror as well. For someone so obsessive about her appearance, it had always puzzled Snow White that the other woman seemed so unsure of herself in private - always asking the mirror if she really was the most beautiful woman in all the land, if she really was the most desirable. What was more, although Snow White had been little more than a child at the time and was now certain that it had been merely the fanciful imaginings of childhood, she distinctly remembered the mirror talking back.

Of course, she was never supposed to see what the former queen had been doing. On the few occasions when she had actually been caught spying, it had meant a severe beating and a swift dismissal. She had honestly never really in her life ever gotten a good look at it and wondered again, as in her youth, why the other woman had been so secretive about the thing. Cautiously, she approached its clean, silvery surface.

That was the first thing that struck her. The huge looking glass did not seem marred by the same coating of dust and bird droppings that blanketed everything else in the room. In fact, had the queen not seen the undisturbed nature of the dust on the stairway leading up here and the generally stagnant condition of the chamber itself, she would have sworn that someone had come and wiped the whole thing down just this morning, so sparkling and pristine did it appear. She looked at herself.

"Mirror?" the queen queried uncertainly, voice echoing in the empty chamber.

She waited, watching it expectantly - Nothing. All she saw in its silvery depths was herself as she had always been - black of hair, pale of feature. Maybe she was a bit heavier than in her youth, and perhaps she had a few more lines and wrinkles with just a touch more gray in her onyx hair, but still she was the same Snow White. She was being silly, and the queen smiled to herself ruefully.

A talking mirror indeed! She thought. *What utter nonsense!* She turned to go.

"Who summons me?"

The deep, onerous voice froze Snow White in her tracks and she turned back toward the looking glass slowly. She could think of nothing at all to say.

"Who is there?" The mirror asked again. The voice seemed to warp and change into something sounding a bit more human. Snow White honestly thought that it seemed vaguely familiar. "Have you returned to me at last, Arglist? It has been so long..."

"Who addresses the Queen?" Snow White asked in reply, trying to put on her most regal sounding voice. She feared that it quavered more than a little bit, however.

"I can barely make out your words, Dearest," The mirror continued plaintively. "Step closer..."

Reluctantly Snow White complied and repeated her question. "Who addresses the Queen?"

"Has it been so long that you've forgotten me, My Love?" The mirror asked dolefully. "It is I as I have ever been since you sealed my spirit in this glass. It is I as I have been ever since the day my body failed me..."

Very slowly beneath the reflection of her own fearful face, a vaguely human form began to coalesce in the mirror's surface. It seemed as if it approached her from very far away, rising up from some great depth. Gradually the shape grew more obvious, the features more clear until she could make out a tall muscular man.

His eyes were so brown that they looked almost black and his hair was darker still. He had strong high cheekbones and a merry sparkle in his eyes. Although the image was of a much younger man than the queen remembered she recognized him immediately and gasped in astonishment.

"So tell me my wife," the man in the mirror commanded good-naturedly.

He set his hand casually against the mirror's surface as if leaning against a window pane. He gave his head a coy toss before continuing with an easy grin.

"How is our daughter? How is our Snow White?"

Chapter 3

The queen fell to her knees and pressed her face and hands against the tall looking glass in dismay. Across all the years and all the struggles, even though decades dead, the evil woman had still found a way to hurt her! What had the hideous old witch done?

"Father!" She cried brokenly clawing at the silvery surface of the mirror. "What has she done to you? I thought you years dead and here I find you trapped in this horrible place in this unnatural existence!"

"Why... Snow White!" The apparition in the glass responded happily. "It is you! I'm so glad you are feeling better. Your stepmother told me of your illness... She did not say it to me, but I knew that she feared you would not survive... But come! That is all over now. Stand before me, my princess, and let me look at you!"

"Father," moaned the queen forlornly. "What is the meaning of this? What are you talking about? I do not understand. How did Arglist imprison you like this? What can I do to help?"

"Where is your mother, by the way?" asked the apparently oblivious king. "I wish to look upon her beautiful face once more... There is only one more beautiful after all..." He added the last with another companionable grin.

"If you mean Arglist, my father, she is dead... many years dead. I myself am no longer the little girl you recall." Snow White met her father's eyes coldly. She was suddenly angry. "My hair is graying. My skin wrinkles and sags and turns to chalk. My eyes grow heavy with the weight of years and lose their sparkle. I am becoming old and she who was your wife and *my* tormentor is long dead. How is it that you remain? What has that *witch* done to you?!"

"Snow White," he chided with a bit of a scowl. He crossed his arms sternly. "I know that you and your stepmother do not always see eye to eye, but please do not refer to her so in my presence. Often have I chastised her as well in your regard. I would that my two pretty girls get along. Can you not manage that for me? May I not have peace in my own home?"

"So often did she come to me in despair at the cruelty of my nobles," he continued. "If I had been able to continue along in body as I once did I might have put an end to it. I think perhaps, she blamed you a little, and that was not fair of course, but she always felt a bit of a failure because of her inability to give me an heir. She deserves your sympathy and understanding my princess, not your ire."

"You always take her side! Why do you love her more than me?!" screamed Snow White viciously as she leapt to her feet. As many years as had passed, the old bitterness she had secretly harbored toward her father came boiling back. "She *lied* father! She kept you from me! She *stole* you from me! That among the other things she did to me to bring me low, are unforgivable! But did you not hear me? She is *dead*! Long dead! And I'm *glad*! She tried to kill me! She tried to *poison* me! Do you care nothing at all about that?

"How many nights did I cry myself to sleep missing you?" Snow White went on, bursting into furious tears. "How many times did I pray fervently that I would wake up from my nightmare, and you and mother would be back beside me! How many nights did I have to cower in fear on a cold stone floor of a pantry dreading the insane whims and unreasoning jealousy of a mad woman? How many beatings, and bruises, and broken bones did I suffer? Yet you tell me to be without ire?!

"You brought that... that *woman* into our home! You took her to your bed! Then you left her with me all by myself, nothing more than a child to deal with her terrible jealousy and hatred! Every morning I awoke! Every morning you were gone! You should have been there! I needed you and you were gone!

"It was all your fault, Father! She made my life *miserable!*" Snow White took a deep breath. Her eyes blazed. "I *hate* her! Why did you leave me all alone? Why did you abandon me?! I was so lonely! I needed you! I *needed* you!!! I... I needed you..." She spluttered off into a bitter silence, able to say no more.

"Indeed..." The shape in the mirror again transformed into a nondescript, vaguely human form. The voice returned to its original otherworldly tones. "As you said yourself, she is long dead... As is he. Wherefore then does this anger spring?"

"You are *not* my father," Snow White breathed in horror taking a staggering step away from the shimmering looking glass.

The insidious device had taken her off her guard. It made her reveal some of her most private emotions, some of the least charitable thoughts in her heart. She had loved her father dearly and never wanted to sully her happy memories of him by admitting her anger and hurt at what he had done to her. The mirror made her say things that she had never revealed to anyone before, not even to Charming. She refocused her outrage on the strange, magical device.

"You are some... some *demon* thing!" She cried accusingly, horrified by the deeply buried anger it had awakened. "What are you trying to do to me? What do you *want* from me?!"

"I am nothing of the sort," scoffed the mirror dismissively, clearly unperturbed by the queen's rage. "And as for what I want - nothing at all! I simply do that which mirrors do. You look in. I show you a reflection of yourself - Nothing more. Your stepmother thought herself beautiful, but I showed her the ugliness that dwelt in her heart as well. She asked me then who there was more beautiful than she and again I showed her. Some people are frightened of their own reflection, I've found. They do not want to examine themselves too closely, for fear of what they will see - For fear of what others might discover. Arglist was such a one, but what of Snow White? Dare you look more deeply?"

"I don't trust you," stated Snow White shakily. "I don't believe you!"

She was not at all sure what to make of this strange device. It was the plaything of a woman she detested – a woman who had gone out of her way to hurt her, to *murder* her even. Its designs were clearly suspect. Her better judgment told her that she should go. She should run away and scream for the guard at the top of her lungs! But she was transfixed. Snow White found that she could not make herself look away.

"Whether you believe me or not is immaterial," the mirror stated flatly. "Your reflection is what your reflection is. Either you will look, or you will not. Either you will believe or you will not. I have but shown you a very small piece of yourself, yet it is one that you have tried to hide. It is but one that causes you pain. You are in pain, are you not?"

Snow White could not answer immediately. She did not want to believe the mirror. Rather she wanted to pick up something heavy and smash the hateful thing into a million pieces. At the same time however, she had to grudgingly admit that she could not fully deny the truth of its words. For over a year she had languished in a melancholic funk. Try though she might, she had not yet discovered how she might drag herself out of it and once again join the legions of the insouciant living, who seemed to blithely flaunt their happiness and contentment under her very nose at every turn. Might this strange arcane device hold some solution to her pain?

The mirror spoke, seemingly in answer to the thought.

"Look within, Snow White," it beckoned emotionlessly. "Look within and see… Or do not, and suffer the lack."

The queen swallowed purposefully. Slowly, wordlessly, and much more tentatively than before, she approached the silvery surface and looked in once again.

Again the vague image beneath the glass solidified into something that looked more real, but at first she could not tell exactly what it was that she beheld. She squinted her eyes and tilted her head curiously. There was a tiny crack of light that followed along the floor to the right then turned at a ninety degree angle to continue upwards as far as she could see. What could it be? Then she gasped. She remembered this.

It was from a time long distant – nearly a lifetime ago. In fact, so deeply buried had the memory been, it felt almost as if she witnessed the events of someone else's life, but no. This ancient moment was hers.

She could not really articulate what happened next, but the world around her seemed suddenly to skew and distort. The dusty room fled from the peripheries of her vision until she beheld nothing but the mirror. It felt almost as if she fell into the glistening surface, much as she might plunge into the crystalline waters of a cold mountain pool or perhaps it was the mirror's gleaming depths that reached out to envelope her. In any case, things were suddenly different. Suddenly, she was no longer simply watching.

***

Snow White nestled deeper into the darkened closet, trying to be as quiet as possible. It would not do to make a noise, because then she would certainly be discovered. She heard footsteps outside her hiding spot and sucked in a quick, panicked breath.

"Snow White?" a voice called softly. "Where are you Snow White? I'm going to find you!"

The little princess did her best to remain silent. She put both hands over her mouth and tightly closed her eyes.

"Come out, come out wherever you are!" the voice crooned. "There's no use in hiding from me – no need to run."

The princess tried to make herself as small as possible, squatting down into a tight little ball. Maybe the voice at the door would go away.

"I always find you, you know," it went on. "Why don't you come out?"

The voice was right in front of the door now. Snow White could even see the speaker's thick black boots through the gap between the bottom of the door and the hard stone flagstones beneath. She held her breath.

"Snow White?" the voice called again. "Snow White? Where... Aha!"

The closet door flew open and Snow White was seized by large, powerful hands. She felt herself lifted from the ground and swung high in the air. The princess squealed.

"There's my little princess!" boomed a deep, friendly voice. He squeezed Snow White and affectionately kissed her cheek.

"Daddy!" she complained seriously. "No! No! No! Your beard tickles! No kisses!"

King Garion laughed long and hard. He squeezed his daughter once more. Then he set her on the floor.

"Little Snow Flake," began Garion kindly as he knelt before her. He met her petulant scowl seriously. "Might I inquire? Why are you hiding in the closet?"

The princess frowned at her little feet, but said nothing.

"Snow White?" King Garion prompted again.

"I don't want to go," Snow White pouted at last. "I want to stay here."

"Could you tell me *why* you do not wish to go?" the king asked patiently.

"No," replied Snow White shortly.

"Why not?" the king again asked with a sigh.

"'Cause you'll get mad at me," mumbled the princess wiping her eye with her tiny fist.

"I don't want you to get mad at me."

"What if I promise not to get mad at you?" her father suggested with another soft grin. "Would you tell me then?"

Snow White bit her lower lip and thought about that for a minute. She looked up at her father suspiciously. "You really promise? Not to get mad? Not even a little bit?"

"Not even a little bit," reassured the king.

"Well, okay then," relented the princess at last. "I don't want to go 'cause I don't want to get a new mommy today. I don't *need* a new mommy. I want to ride my pony."

Her father chuckled. "I know you love your pony, my princess, but how about if we ride him when we get back?" Snow White bit her lip again and looked down at the floor.

"No." she said at last. "I just don't want to go."

"What's wrong, Little Snowflake," he asked, brushing a stray hair away from her pretty face. "I've told you every day for a month that we would be bringing your new mommy home today. You didn't forget did you?"

Snow White continued to stare at her toes. "No…"

"What's wrong then?"

"I don't *want* a new mommy, Daddy!" she whined at last. "I want my old mommy. I *liked* my old mommy!"

"Don't you like your new mommy too?" The king pressed gently. "You told me you thought she was pretty."

"Yeah," answered the little girl considering, "but my real mommy was good at telling stories. Is the new mommy good at telling stories?"

"I don't know, Snowflake," her father answered earnestly.

"And my real mommy was good at holding me," Snow White went on critically. "Will the new mommy be good at holding me?"

"I think she might be with some practice," he answered.

"And my real mommy played with me and gave me kisses," the little girl went on. "Will the new mommy play with me and give me kisses? Not prickly kisses!" she added as her father leaned towards her. He smiled and straightened

"I'm sure she wouldn't mind it if you asked her, Snow White," he replied with a chuckle.

"Why can't Mommy come home, Daddy?" the princes blurted, looking up at her father intensely. "Doesn't she want to see us? Is she angry at us?"

Tears sprang to the king's eyes. He picked up Snow White and held her close.

"No My Little One," he murmured. "Your mother isn't angry at us."

"Then why can't she come home, Daddy?" pressed the little princess. "Why can't she come home and play with me?"

"She just… She just got called away early," replied Garion huskily.

"Can we visit her?" asked the princess hopefully. "Mommy will be happy to see me! She will love my pretty blue dress! It swirls when I dance. See?"

Snow White squirmed to get down. Then she spun in a circle to demonstrate and nearly fell over as she lost her balance. Her father provided a steadying hand.

"Mommy would be very happy to see you, Little One," the king sighed, "but that just isn't possible…"

"Why not?" the princess pressed.

Garion sighed with a hint of frustration showing in his voice. He ran a harried hand through his thick black hair and answered in a rush.

"When people…" her father began. "When they go where your mother went, they can never come back, no matter how much they want to."

"Why did Mommy go away, Daddy?" Snow White asked sadly. "Why did she leave us all alone?"

"I think I've already explained this Snow White," the king replied with a little more irritation showing through. "When God calls someone away, they have to go and that's that! It's just like when I tell my subjects to do something. They have to do it. Your mother did not choose to leave us. It was just her time…"

"Well," replied Snow White quickly, brightening at a sudden thought. "Could *you* tell God to bring her back? You're the king."

"Little Snow White," the king began patiently resting his hands heavily on her tiny shoulders. "Even kings have their masters. There are some things that even kings cannot command."

"Oh," said Snow White sadly.

"But your mother is in a wonderful place," the king explained. A quiver came to his voice. "It's a place where she will never hurt anymore or be sad or lonely… And someday we will be able to join her there."

"Daddy," Snow White asked softly and brushed his cheek with her little hand. "Why are you crying?"

"Because Snow White," her father answered haltingly, squeezing her tight once more. "*I* am sad and lonely, and I don't want to be anymore."

"Oh," Snow White thought for a moment. "I can make you happy, Daddy! You will not be lonely with me!" She twirled in her pretty blue dress again.

"You make me *very* happy, Snow White," her father chuckled. "And you always will, but sometimes... Sometimes big people need special time with other big people. When you're big you'll want that time too."

"Oh," said Snow White. She looked at her father seriously. "Will the new mommy make you happy, Daddy? Will the new mommy make you not be lonely anymore?"

"I believe that she will, Snow White."

"Okay," answered the princess. "I do not want you to be sad, Daddy. We can go get the new mommy for you, but... I still like my *real* mommy." She whispered the last part.

"Thank you, Snow White." Her father smiled at her.

"Daddy?"

"Yes, Snow White?"

"Can I still ride my pony when we get home?"

"Of course, Little One," the king responded indulgently.

"Daddy?"

"Yes, Snow White?"

"I'm glad you found me," she confided in a whisper. "It was a little scary in there all by myself. Will you promise to stay with me forever and ever? Will you promise to never go away like Mommy?"

"I promise to love you forever and ever, Snow White," replied Garion. "And I'm not going anywhere for a very, very long time. Now let's go fetch your new mommy! I'm sure you and the Lady Arglist will get along *famously*. I bet you'll be best friends in no time!"

Daddy did not mean to lie.

Chapter 4

Snow White staggered away from the magical looking glass shaking her head in confusion. She looked around. Where had Daddy gone? Were they not about to go outside to the royal carriage? Was the captain not going to order up her father's men into two long, straight lines flanked on either side by a troop of his knights, trumpets blaring, flags fluttering in the warm spring breeze? She was going to sit on his lap and look out the window as the kingdom of Gutefehia passed her by outside on their way to meet the new mommy together.

Wait. No... She thought. *That's not right.*

She raised her hands to her spinning head and gasped. Snow White stared at her hands. They seemed far too old and veiny to really be hers. She looked at herself in the boiling depths of the mirror. Who was that old lady? What just happened?

"I am impressed, Snow White," the mirror rumbled. "It has been long indeed since someone dared to gaze so long ago and deeply."

The queen shook her head again and suddenly remembered who and where she was. She regarded the shapeless figure in the glass suspiciously.

"What just happened?" she asked in bewilderment. "I... I was a little girl. That was my father. I mean..." she trailed off at a loss. "I mean it was *really* him. I heard his voice and he... he held me and he hugged me. I felt him pick me up!"

"I already told you," sighed the mirror impatiently. "Of *course* it was really him. Or I suppose rather..." It paused considering. "It was your true reflection of him."

"What do you mean?" asked the queen in puzzlement. "What do you mean 'my true reflection'?"

"I am a *mirror*," the mirror repeated. "All I can do is reflect that which is already within you. Everything you see is already a part of you. Were that not so, I could not show it."

"Then why look?" asked the queen. "What's the point? If I know everything you can show me already, then what purpose is there in..."

"I did not say that you *knew* everything already," interrupted the mirror slyly. "Only that the visions I can reveal are already within you. It isn't the same thing at all. Much of your heart remains hidden, even from the ones you love most – even from yourself. If you wish, I will show you, much like now, things you have forgotten - events of long ago. Other times, I will show you things that you knew deep inside, but never fully realized or articulated with word or thought. I can give you clarity. Then sometimes, only sometimes, I will reveal those, dark, secret things from the murkiest depths of your own heart that you never wanted anyone else to know about or indeed, things you have refused to admit even to yourself. Those are the visions of greatest value, but also greatest danger, for they are the inescapable horrors of your own making. You cannot run away from yourself.

"So what say you, Queen Snow White?" The mirror went on. "Dare you see more? Will you delve even deeper, or do you fear what I will discover inside of you?"

Snow White still felt uneasy. She feared this magical device. Could she truly trust something that had been so dear to a woman who had damaged her so?

The image in the looking glass changed again and Snow White cried out. An undeniably beautiful woman gazed back at her imperiously. She had fine, high cheek bones and large luminous eyes. Her figure was slim but womanly, tiny waste encircled by a beautiful golden belt. Her amble bosom threatened to erupt from the top of her dangerously low-cut bodice and her hair was long and sable, tied back in a severe bun, but all that did was emphasize the loveliness of her perfectly painted face. All of these exceptional features were obscured by a vengeful mask of rage, however. It was an expression with which Snow White was all too familiar. With a scream, she felt herself falling again.

***

Snow White paused with her fist raised. She did not like coming here. It was cold in the corridor and the young princess could see her breath. She shivered.

The rough, burlap sack that she wore as a dress, and that had apparently once contained oats judging by the faded labeling, was scratchy against her soft skin. It provided absolutely no warmth. She had grown over the summer and now it was uncomfortably tight across her chest and getting short enough that she was constantly pulling it down at the hem to avoid exposing herself. The princess yawned and looked out an open window to her left. It was still pitch black outside. Dawn would not come for several more hours yet.

Mrs. Maloche had minced no words. She had been apologetic but brisk when she approached Snow White's thin pallet in the pantry of the main kitchen. She was sorry about waking her at such an ungodly hour, but her stepmother, the regent, required her presence immediately.

The stout little housekeeper was nice in her way, Snow White supposed, but just like everyone else, kept her distance. She could not risk being seen by Lady Arglist as getting too friendly with the sad little princess. Everyone knew what happened to those who did.

There was Ewald the stable boy who let Snow White help him brush the horses for a few days last spring. He had been found in a stall late one evening with his brains bashed out. Arglist declared that it must have happened when the princess' childhood pony, Struppig, had reared and kicked him. No matter that the ancient animal could barely walk from the stall to the coral anymore, Arglist had still seen the animal destroyed for the alleged offence.

Then there was Stina, the chamber maid – a pretty, young thing from the country, popular with all the boys on the staff. Snow White especially remembered her pleasant smile and ready laugh. She had mysteriously fallen down a flight of stairs and broken both her legs just a day after sneaking the princess extra blankets from the laundry.

Hobert, the blacksmith's apprentice, was summoned away late one night, just hours after talking with the princess for a few minutes in the courtyard and never seen again. Horst, the kitchen assistant who had once brought her a half-eaten sweet cake, discarded from the regent's table had been horribly scalded in a "kitchen accident" the next day. Poor Resi, the chambermaid who was only about a year older than Snow White herself had been beaten and cast out of the castle for "stealing" food a mere week after she decided to make her bed alongside the neglected princess. That one stung Snow White the most. She had really liked the perky, red-headed girl and had even dared to dream that they might become friends.

There had been others too, of course, punished for this or beaten for that if they dared share too many words with the princess, so that now the Castle Wolfejager servants avoided her like the plague. Snow White did her best to stay out of their way too. It broke her heart to bits every time Arglist decided to hurt someone on her behalf and she had decided long ago that she could not bear that on her conscience any longer. The result was that she led a sad, solitary existence.

Snow White had to fend for herself. She was never allowed water to bathe and was always dirty and hungry. She generally drank from the rain barrel in the court yard or the horse trough in the corral. The princess was even reduced to stealing food from the kitchens to feed herself or pilfering sacks from the storage room when no one was looking to fashion make-shift clothing. However, to be fair, no one was really watching that hard.

Everyone saw her, but made as if they did not. She moved among them, but everyone acted as if she was not there at all. It made her want to stand in the middle of the courtyard and scream at the top of her lungs; "Here I am! See me! See me!" But of course, she would never *really* do that. Arglist's retribution for making such a disturbance would have been swift and terrible. Instead, the princess made every effort to be invisible, like a little ghost haunting the shadowy corners of her own castle.

Snow White balked at the doorway, fist still poised to knock. The thudding and smashing of crockery was clearly audible within and she heard voices – loud, angry voices. One, the princess did not recognize, but she could easily make out Arglist's indignant shrieking. Clearly her stepmother was furious. God only knew what the woman wanted this time.

The regent summoned her regularly – usually late at night or early in the morning like it was now. Sometimes it was to brush her highness' hair or clean up her highness' spilled food or drink. Sometimes it was to polish her highness's brass, or scrub her highness' floor. Sometimes it was to take her highness' dirty clothing to the laundry or any number of other, menial chores. Often, Arglist would want her to do nothing at all but stand in the corner being quiet and unobtrusive. Though still a child of only twelve, Snow White suspected that the main reason the regent summoned her was simply to demonstrate to her and everyone else that she could and that the princess had no choice but to obey.

Snow White sighed in resignation. There was no point in dragging it out. Arglist would only become more enraged at her dallying and make the whole unpleasant ordeal that much more miserable. It was best to just get it over with. She rapped three times on the heavy door.

It swung open so abruptly that the princess was nearly knocked backwards down the stairs. Snow White was grabbed by the front of her makeshift smock and pulled forcefully into the room.

"Where have you been, you little slut?!" screamed Lady Arglist. "Do you expect me to wait on you all night? I'll teach you the meaning of haste!"

The regent slapped Snow White hard enough across the face that she saw black spots and fell to the lush, red carpet covering the floor of the regent's apartments. Arglist dragged the whimpering little girl back to her feet, twisting her arm painfully behind her. Snow White could only gape. Arglist was never exactly tender with her, but this behavior seemed extreme even for her unreasonable stepmother

"What did I do!?" wailed the aghast princess, clutching at her stinging face. The look in Arglist's eyes was terrifying. Snow White had never seen her so angry. "Please, your Highness! You're hurting me!"

The furious noblewoman twisted even harder.

"Hurting you?! How dare you presume to command me!" she screamed. "When I choose to hurt you I promise that you shall know it! When I summon you I expect you to be here *instantly*! I will not be made to wait like a peasant begging alms on the street corner by some shiftless waif! Do you think me some peasant, arrogant girl?! Do you?! Do you think because your father was the king that you are too good to do as you're told by the likes of me?!" She shook the princess until Snow White was dizzy.

"No, Highness! I..."

"Silence!" thundered Arglist. She paused in her rant to stare straight into Snow White's eyes. She examined her carefully, as if evaluating her every feature and blemish. Arglist continued silently staring with an unfathomable expression on her face for a very long time. It made Snow White squirm, but she dared not look away.

"Do you think yourself *pretty*, princess?" Arglist dangerously breathed at last. "Do you think yourself *beautiful*?"

The unexpected question took her off guard.

"I... I... I... I..." Snow White stammered, not knowing what to say in the face of the woman's strange behavior.

"Let me disabuse you, princess," Arglist snarled. "You are *not*. You are an ugly little urchin cast upon me like a millstone around my neck - The spawn of a noble sire and a hideous, weakling, nothing of a mother!"

She yanked the princess violently across the room by her awkwardly twisted arm. There was a loud pop and Snow White shrieked as blazing pain shot suddenly through her shoulder. Arglist shoved her to the floor. Then the regent dug around in a nearby wardrobe for a moment before advancing on the terrified princess with a long, sharp knife.

"Please, your Highness!" Snow White begged piteously, her good arm raised defensively before her. Her other trailed along uselessly at her side on the floor as she scrambled awkwardly backwards. She only stopped when her back pressed up against the wall in the far corner of the room. Terrified tears gushed from saucer-like eyes as Arglist stalked purposely toward her.

"Please don't!" Snow White wailed. "No! Don't hurt me! I'm sorry! *I'm sorry*! Please don't hurt me! I know I'm ugly. You are beautiful and I am ugly! I never said I was pretty! I never said! Please, Majesty! *Please* don't! NO!!!"

Arglist grabbed her by the hair and pulled her to her feet as she raised the glittering blade. With a snarl, the furious noble woman began viciously slashing and hacking. She chopped great chunks out of Snow White's hair until it littered the floor and obscured the carpet beneath. The uneven mess left on the princess' head stuck out in every direction. Again Arglist struck her and once more Snow White collapsed to the floor. The regent kept hitting her and hitting her until Snow White's face was a purple mass of bruises. Then the enraged woman straightened to kick the piteously shrieking girl with sharply pointed, hard-toed leather boots.

After quite some time, Arglist finally wearied from her exertions. Breathing heavily, she dragged the whimpering princess to her feet. Snow White could barely stand and had such difficulty opening her eyes that she could hardly see. Her stepmother opened the heavy oaken door of her chambers and thrust her out into the hallway. She watched coldly as Snow White tumbled down the stairs to the first landing below.

"You will *never* be as beautiful as I!" She hissed viciously. "No man will *ever* want you the way they desire me! You will never even come *close*! You will *never* replace me! I will protect what is

31

mine, do you hear? I am queen and ever will be! Me! Now, away with you! Trouble me no more! The sight of you sickens me…" As the door began to swing closed, Snow White heard the horrible woman muttering to herself. "Who's most beautiful now?!"

The door slammed shut and Snow White was left alone in a quaking heap at the bottom of the stairs. She stared up at the cold, grey ceiling above. Her face throbbed. It felt swollen and puffy to the touch. Her nose was bleeding heavily from both nostrils, soaking the front of her burlap dress. Her right arm felt like a useless dead weight at her side and her ribs pulsed with screaming pain. She hurt all over. With her left hand, Snow White felt her butchered hair and began sobbing, but even that hurt. It was difficult to breathe.

Snow White continued to whimper in a thin, raspy wheeze as she used her good arm to painfully turn herself over. Then she clawed her way up the rough granite wall of the corridor and leaned against it until she thought she could move without collapsing. Supporting herself heavily on the wall of the stairwell, she limped heavy, staggering steps, back down the stairs and on to the main kitchens. She moved very, very slowly.

When she entered, the room was bustling. The first shift had already arrived and preparations for serving breakfast were well underway. All activity abruptly ceased and everyone fell silent in horror when they caught sight of her, but no one made any move to help. Snow White said nothing; head lowered in embarrassment, shamed by all of those wide, aghast eyes upon her. Wordlessly, she hobbled her way back to the pantry and collapsed in a heap onto her thin mat where she lay still.

A little while later, Mrs. Maloche looked in on her and a furious, whispered conversation ensued at the door of the pantry that Snow White could not understand. After perhaps a half to three quarters of an hour, one of the young men who worked in the stables crept into the storage room as if he was there to rob it. He barely spoke as he hastily set her badly dislocated shoulder. It made Snow White shriek in agony as the joint popped back into place. Then he left without a word, as if afraid that Arglist might suddenly appear out of thin air to catch him in his nefarious deed. The princess was left alone, battered and bloodied in the lonely little room. No one else offered any assistance and nothing more about the incident was ever mentioned by anyone ever again.

The days went by and Snow White's injuries healed. The distance between herself and the other people who dwelt in Castle Wolfejager only increased after her beating. A small blessing was that Arglist did not call her again for quite some time, but eventually call her she did. Snow White never did find out what it was she had done to provoke her stepmother's fit or indeed what would provoke any of the others to come that would be nearly as bad.

Her miserable isolation and loneliness continued. Could it really have been four more years that she languished there? It seemed like such a very long time when she thought about it, but then again disconnected from her somehow, almost as if it had happened to a different person. Maybe in some ways it had.

Chapter 5

Snow White came back to herself slowly. She found herself sitting in the floor with her knees tucked up under her chin, rocking back and forth, and cowering like a beaten dog. She vaguely felt throbbing pain in her face and in her shoulder, but it quickly faded. She shook herself, leapt to her feet and rounded on the mirror in a fury.

"Why would you do such a thing to me?!" she demanded angrily. "Why would you make me relive that? What sick pleasure do you take from witnessing my misery? How *dare* you torture me with her! Is it that you still do your foul mistress' bidding? For if that be the case, then you shall be disappointed! My husband put an end to her vile scheming years ago! Your assaults upon me are to no avail! I will see you ripped from that wall and ground to a powder for this! I..."

"Did you hear nothing of what I told you before?" interrupted the amorphous figure in the mirror unexcitedly. "I did *nothing* to you. Everything that you experience in my depths comes from within you yourself! If you feel pain, it is not I who is causing it! Do you not understand? Arglist abused you. She broke you. She tormented and reviled you and to this day you carry those old scars and hurts. Me torment you? You torment yourself! I am nothing more than a tool whereby you may see yourself more clearly. This pain, it is old and it is deep, but it comes from within you and it haunts you still."

Snow White did not reply, but closed her eyes, slowed her breathing, and gradually managed to regain her composure.

"You have no idea," she murmured at last shaking her head sadly. "You have no concept of what it was like. How much she hurt me, how often... How utterly alone I was! Every day was a misery. Every morning my only hope was for night and oblivious sleep. I could not even *dream*, because every one of them was a nightmare. In every one, *she* was waiting for me!"

"But it ended, didn't it?" pressed the mirror softly. "Horrible as it was, this was long, long ago, was it not? Surely, your life has not been uninterrupted misery from that day until this, has it?"

Snow White did not immediately respond. Her first impulse was to deny what the mirror said, but she knew that was just her dejection talking. If she was honest, yes, things had indeed improved and indeed, improved quite dramatically. She could not deny the years of happiness she had certainly enjoyed, but much like this old pain, that joy too seemed disconnected from her. Had that really been her life? Had there really been a time when this melancholic despair had not been an all pervasive part of herself? She no longer feared beatings and abuse, true, but the loneliness she felt now was very near those old isolated feelings in the kitchen pantry.

She felt abandoned after her father died and now realized that she felt very much the same way about Charming's death. What was worse, she now recognized that she actually blamed the two people she had loved most for her loneliness, which then made her feel guilty and even more miserable. She felt tears coming again.

What a broken mess I am! She thought forlornly.

"Snow White," the mirror called softly, extracting her gently from her unhappy musings. "There was happiness also. You know there was. Do you not remember? You grieve now for your weakness, but just recall the adversity you did indeed conquer! It was a long and bitter road you took. There were few who could have even attempted the journey you completed. How did that come about? Do you not recall?"

"Charming," she breathed, tears again spilling down her cheeks. That was the answer. He had been her champion, her savior. It was he who had rescued her from years of misery and despair. He was her happiness. Now both were gone.

"Your husband might have been a catalyst, yes," the mirror conceded. "But do you not remember what you had to endure to find that happiness together? You overcame much."

Snow White shook her head stubbornly. She did not want to contemplate the question too carefully. She had no desire to experience any more of the unpleasantness she had just endured. The mirror seemed to sense her reticence.

"Yes, you were weak once," it murmured, "You were helpless and miserable but despite everything that was done to you, you did discover strength. Can you not remember it? How did it come about before?"

"I did nothing." Snow White sighed, sinking to her knees and staring down at her hands. "It was all Charming. It was he who saved me. He…"

"Do you *really* believe that to be true?" interrupted the mirror incredulously. "No one achieves anything all alone. There are always other actors in any success or failure, of course, but I think you sell yourself short! Tell me you recall of what I speak! Remember the strength you have shown!"

Snow White sighed. She did not feel very strong at the moment. She felt tragic and dejected. The mirror's words were actually making her feel worse. Yes, her life had been horrible before, much as it was horrible now. Charming had saved her from that misery once, but now he was gone like her mother and father before him. Her saviors had all gone away. She closed her eyes tightly and felt the tears coming again.

"You know *nothing*," gasped the queen bitterly.

"I cannot force you to do anything," the mirror pressed undeterred, "but I do know this: If you would have joy again, you must recall how you first found it and that answer lies within you. If you would find strength again you must likewise recall how you discovered it before. It lies beyond the pain. Have you not said yourself that you no longer remember how you might be happy again? Look deeply, see what you were, and you may! What you experience now are but shadows of things that have already been. There is nothing here that can hurt you but you yourself."

The queen clinched her eyes shut. Yes, she wanted to find the joy long absent in her life. She wanted to be happy. She wanted to feel strong again, but she had already endured so much pain! Could she tolerate yet more? Was it even worth it? Was it not better just to lock it away and pretend none of it had ever happened? Was it not better to simply forget everything and just start over? The mirror seemed to read her thoughts.

"But Snow White," it pressed softly. "You know there is no forgetting, not really. What happens, happens. The past is the past and your past is ever a part of you! Only by facing it can you truly leave it behind. Otherwise, it will ever intrude upon your present..." The queen said nothing, but exhaled deeply. Then she swallowed. Very slowly, Snow White raised her head. She looked into the swirling depths.

This time the image was dark and strange. It was almost as if she gazed across a chasm, wide and deep. She felt as if she stood alone on the edge of a precipitous gorge, filled with despair at the impossibility of her predicament, but knowing that her only choice was to descend into its shadowy depths, cross the unseen rocky path at its bottom, and pull herself out once more on the other side. She had felt this way once before.

***

Snow White stared into the darkness irresolutely. Rain poured down in torrents and the howling wind threatened to steal the cloak from about her slender shoulders. Thunder boomed and crashed while lightening danced and arched across the sky. She balked at the gaping gates of Castle Wolfejager. Her time was short.

They were already looking for her. She knew she should go. She knew she should flee into the night and not stop until she dropped from exhaustion, but was still strangely reluctant.

She thought back on the frantic events of the last half hour or so in amazement. How could things change so much so quickly?

It had actually been Mrs. Maloche who roused her. That in itself was nothing unusual. Typically, whenever Arglist concocted some new and ridiculous method whereby she might degrade and abuse the young princess, it was the portly house keeper's task to deliver the unhappy news. In all times past, Mrs. Maloche had been curt and business-like, delivering the message in as few clipped syllables as possible, but this time was different.

Snow White had woken suddenly to urgent shaking and thunder rolling in the distance. The elderly servant's eyes were wide and fearful and the princess quickly recognized that the woman was still dressed in her night gown. Her generally neat and carefully coifed grey hair hung freely about her shoulders and she wore no make-up. When she noted that Snow White's eyes were open, Mrs. Maloche quickly shoved a bulging burlap sack into the princess' chest.

"Get up, girl!" she hissed in a panicked whisper. "You must leave! Get out of Castle Wolfejager right now! Leave and never come back!"

"Wha... huh?" Snow White mumbled sleepily. "What do you...?"

"There's no time!" interrupted the frantic servant. "You must go! The Regent is in a *horrible* rage! She just... just... pitched poor little Mitzi..." her voice caught in her throat and she sniffled.

"…Pitched her right out that high tower window of hers! Then she called for you and for her huntsman. I *heard* her!"

Snow White gasped, but the full impact of horrific news was not quick to register in her sleep muddled brain. She shook her head helplessly.

"I don't under…"

"You must not linger, Your Highness!" Mrs. Maloche pressed insistently. "This man… it is not beasts he hunts. He is a horrible man – a murderer and a… a… a *demon*! He is little more than Arglist's assassin and executioner. He kills for pleasure! I heard the Regent myself, Princess! She is sending him for you. Arglist has grown bold indeed. She fears no retribution or chastisement anymore. She means to *kill* you! You must not dally! You must flee!"

A great knot of dread quickly formed in the pit of Snow White's stomach. She was afraid certainly, but not exactly shocked. There had been numerous occasions when she had feared for her life in her step-mother's presence. In fact, now that she thought about it, she was unsure what had stopped the horrible woman from ending her before. She nodded quickly and leapt to her feet.

Snow White started to go, no idea in her head but to run and hide! …but she stopped in confusion. *Go where? Hide where?!* She thought in a panic. There was no place in the castle where the Regent would not find her. Mrs. Maloche seemed to read her expression.

"You must *go*!" Mrs. Maloche repeated intensely. "Run for the gates, princess! Go where the regent cannot find you!"

Still Snow White hesitated. Could she really just flee into the night? Could she really abandon the only home she had ever known with barely a thought? What would she do once she left? Mrs. Maloche again accurately read the princess' reticence in her aghast face.

"Fear not, Princess Snow White," she reassured intensely. "You will not be alone – neither here nor outside these walls. There are still those among us who loved your father well. The gates will be open for you, I promise!" Then she swallowed and stopped. She looked down at the floor. When she continued, her voice was tiny and ashamed.

"Forgive me, princess," she breathed. "You should never have been made to suffer like this. Long ago, I should have…"

Just then a clamor of shouting voices came to their ears from deeper in the castle. Mrs. Maloche's eyes grew wide.

"Go now!" she commanded. "There is no more time. I will send them another way! I will tell them you heard them and ran towards the west wing! You must get to the gates! Flee into the countryside! Arglist is well hated among the common folk, Princess. Your people will aide you, but go quickly! Run into the night and do not stop even with the breaking of the dawn!" She gave Snow White a little push towards the door.

After she was actually moving, the princess wasted no time. She sprinted out of the kitchen and through the deserted laundry, grabbing a handy cloak on her way. She then rushed down hallways and corridors and dashed across the darkened courtyard to stand just where she now found herself - cowering in the shadows beside the gaping gates of Castle Wolfejager, drenched by a heavy rain, frightened almost to distraction by cacophonous thunder and blinding lightning, and sorely divided over whether to abide or to flee.

Behind her was misery and pain to which she knew there was no retreat. Death dogged her heals. At her feet however, was a path of darkness, fear, and uncertainty. Where would she go? She knew nothing of the hinterlands of her kingdom. In fact, she had not once been allowed outside of Castle Wolfejager since her father died nearly five years ago. There was nothing for her beyond this gate, but the fearful unknown.

She did not have to go, Snow White thought suddenly. She could still run and hide somewhere on the grounds. Arglist's rage, as bad as it was tonight, would surely pass. It always did. Snow White was already wet, cold, and miserable without setting so much as her big toe outside of the gates. Her life was certainly not blissful here, but at least she had food, clean water, and a warm, dry place to sleep.

Lightning illuminated the sky brilliantly and the thunder crashed again. Back along the walls of the inner keep she could briefly see the silhouettes of frantic soldiers rushing here and there in the downpour. The angry voices in the castle seemed louder suddenly.

Why soldiers?

Her step mother had never sent soldiers after her before. All the soldiers she had any experience with had been hard, grim men, but had never done her ill. They had always let her be. What would they do if they found her now? She wondered suddenly. What would Arglist do?

Would the regent curse her? Snow White was well used to that. It would not be so bad. Of course, might Arglist not instead beat her with a strap? She did that often enough. It hurt certainly, but the pain usually faded soon after. Would her step mother kick her and punch her until her bones were broken and her pretty face swollen and purple? That had happened a good half dozen times or more. Maybe, Arglist would dump scalding water over her head. That had *really* hurt. Her step mother had done that twice.

Snow White scowled suddenly and stared out the open gate into the darkness.

No, she thought determinedly. *No more. I have had enough.*

She did not deserve Arglist's abuse. Snow White was a *princess* for God's sake! Did that count for nothing? Her father had never treated even criminals and brigands the way her step mother abused her. No more! She was tired of the curses, berating, and name calling, sick of the beatings and lashings and hair pulling, and well over the constant humiliation, isolation, and fear.

Never again.

Even if Arglist stilled her rage this very moment, dressed her in silks and satins and sat her upon her father's throne. Even if she bowed down at her feet and swore fealty right this instant and promised never to become cross ever again, Snow White was done with her.

It was funny really. It seemed so clear now. She had always been nearly petrified of her step mother. Snow White had always feared her down to the deepest fibers of her being, but looking out this dark, open door into the night, shivering with cold and soaked by rain, she realized that she feared Arglist no more.

Arglist's domain was here, but out there… There in the great and trackless lands beyond the place of Snow White's birth were a multitude of houses whose walls had never reverberated with Arglist's indignant shrieking. There were countless mountains and valleys that had never rung with the echoes of her step mother's furious tantrums. There were carpets and floors that had never been dampened by Snow White's spilled blood or bitter tears.

Yes, there was danger outside these walls. Yes, there was uncertainty and fear, but there was also freedom. Far across this darkened plain, beyond the sound of Arglist's shrill voice and the reach of her grasping hands, albeit faintly, Snow White thought she glimpsed the feeble gleam of hope.

Hope for what exactly, she did not know, but it was undeniable. Somewhere before her in the unknowable future at the end of this dark and secret road at her feet was at least a vague inkling that things might somehow, some way be different - be better. Somehow her fortunes might change and she might finally know a life free from fear and pain, but only if she was willing to move forward.

Snow White took a deep breath, closed her eyes, and took a single, deliberate step beyond the threshold of the great iron gates of Castle Wolfejager. She opened her eyes. After that one difficult step, the next was easier and the one after that simpler still. Her pace quickened and her legs pumped. The angry voices behind her faded in the storm and as she finally ducked out of the rain and into the shelter of the first trees at the fringes of the surrounding forest, she realized for the very first time that, come what may, at last she was free. At last, Princess Snow White was the master of her own fate and her soul reveled in that freedom as she strode resolutely onward - out of her old life and boldly into her indiscernible future.

Chapter 6

"It was very difficult for you to make that choice," the mirror commented mildly. "You could have stayed and nothing would have ever been any different. Instead, you made a choice to change your life. You decided that you would no longer be ruled by your fear."

"I fled for my life," Snow White scoffed shaking her head with a bitter chuckle. "You make it sound like some grand, brave thing. What nobility is there in running away? Even deer and rabbits manage it when pursued by the wolf or even the rat when chased by a tabby or stoat."

"Snow White," countered the mirror with some exasperation finally showing faintly through. "Unlike the rabbit or doe you mention, you had a choice. You chose to flee. You could have remained. Perhaps you were right. Maybe you could have hidden in the storage rooms or an abandoned hall, or an empty tower or belfry. Maybe you could have gone down into the dungeons or wine cellars until Arglist's fury had run its course. It is possible that you could have gone on for years and years more just as you always had – living like a beggar and a thief in your own home. But you did not choose that path. You chose the difficult road. You chose the path of greatest risk and uncertainty, but it was also the path that led you to happiness. Do you not see? Arglist thought herself your master. She thought you cowed and harmless, but you proved her wrong. You *escaped* her."

"Escaped her?" countered Snow White in disbelief. "Is that what I did?" She shuttered. "I remember the outcome quite differently."

Silence stretched briefly between them. Behind her, a pigeon cooed softly in its nest and ruffled its feathers before settling. The breeze through the open window tossed and tousled her long, soft hair.

"You paid a price for your choice," the mirror stated at last, "and yes, it was a very high price, but do you regret it? Why were you willing to chance Arglist's displeasure? You knew what she was capable of. You saw her narcissism and brutality daily, and yet you chose to chance her rage.

Snow White did not reply

"You are no scurrying rat!" it exclaimed. "Rather, you found the strength to defy her and wagered your life in the off chance that you might be able to change your lot for the better. Why do you insist on being so stubborn? Why do you deliberately choose to ignore the resilience and determination that you have clearly shown? You knew that your choice might lead to your death and yet you made it anyway. Why?"

Snow White still did not answer. She was yet unconvinced, feeling decidedly weak and alone, but could not deny that a single word kept echoing in her brain in unconscious answer to the mirror's question. It was "hope".

It had been hope which pushed her out those gates that stormy night to flee her ancestral home. It was hope that led her to risk everything so that she might have even a small opportunity to discover any slight degree of happiness and serenity in her future.

What do I hope for now? She mused. *Have I really become so different?* Snow White had to admit that she had not pondered either of those questions in quite some time.

That desire of her youth - that yearning for something better, something more - was not unlike the longing she felt now, she realized. She wanted her continued existence to be more than it was just as much today as in her turbulent childhood. It was that same amorphous desire to do something, *anything* to better her situation that compelled her to gaze yet again into the magical looking glass.

"Very well, Mirror," the queen murmured at last. "Show me what you will. I am ready."

She stared into the glass grimly. This time she was sure she knew what she would see, what she would be forced to pay. The price of her beautiful life with her prince had been very high but, she suddenly understood, she would gladly pay it again. As she let the mirror take her, the queen steeled herself, knowing with certainty that indeed, again pay she would.

***

Snow White lurched and shook on the dusty ground outside the little forest cottage. Birds sang in the trees around her. A gentle breeze rustled gold, bronze, and vermillion boughs and the sun was bright and warm. Late flowers perfumed the air. The splendor of the beautiful autumn day contrasted starkly with the chaos of pain wracking her body.

Sharp rocks and bits of jagged gravel tore at her soft skin as she twisted and contorted on her side in the middle of the narrow country lane. Her feet aimlessly kicked and her heels dug and tore ineffectually at the dry turf. The pain in her stomach was terrible and the convulsions in her abdomen threatened to tear her apart. It felt as though whatever evil spirit had been contained in that single bite of shiny, red fruit was trying to claw its way out of her belly.

She wanted to scream, but found that she could not. The only sound she produced was an awful gurgling, gasping choke. Her mouth gaped and her swollen tongue lolled sickly. Her eyes bulged even as they rolled back in her head and her twisted fingers clawed ineffectually at the azure sky. Erfreut tried to hold her spasming body still, but was only successful in that he kept her turned so that she did not choke on her own vomit. It was getting harder and harder to breath. By God, what had the old hag given her!

"It's no good, Grantig!" the youngest of the seven little men cried in a panic. "I just don't know what else to do! Go find Artz! He'll know something!"

"He could be anywhere!" shouted the elder dwarf in reply. "He'll be well into the middle of his rounds by now! I don't even know where to begin!"

"Head back toward the mine by the main road," Erfreut urgently directed. "And scream bloody murder every step of the way! Wake the very dead until you find 'em. Go, man! Go! She's turnin' blue!"

Grantig wasted no time and soon his short legs were pumping in a frenzy of terror. His shrill voice echoed through the forest and his panicked shouting could be heard long after he had disappeared from sight.

"Come on, Snowy," begged Erfreut desperately. "Stay with me, lass. Help's on the way!"

The little man said something else, but Snow White did not understand it. All she could hear was the labored pounding of her own heart and the same panicked thought echoing over and over again in her brain.

I don't want to die! I don't want to die!

Every muscle felt as though it was being twisted into painful knots and she had no control over any of them. She was a prisoner in her own body. The agony in her belly was terrible and the seizures wracking her slight frame threatened to shake her to pieces. Her intestines evacuated noisily and she violently threw up again, certain that her internal organs must surely be spilling out all over the ground beside her. Her tongue felt thick and ungainly, almost completely filling her gaping mouth. She clawed in futility at her face and throat, but could not clear her airway enough to breathe. Black spots started to form around the edges of her vision and her lungs began to burn.

Oh God, Please! She prayed frantically. *Not after everything I've been through! I can't die! Not Now! Please, not now!*

Her muscles twisted so tightly that she thought they surely must snap her bones in two. The weight on her chest, that already felt onerous, increased making her feel that her breast might literally explode. Just when she was sure that she could endure no more, she mercifully blacked out.

*

The void stretch away from her in every direction, but then again it did not. There was no direction – no up or down or forward or back. There was nothing at all, neither body nor substance, light nor dark, but then again somehow there was also *everything*.

Snow White knew that she was not asleep, but was equally certain she was not awake either. It was like struggling through a thick fog. She was sure she heard voices, but could not make them out, as if they came from a very great distance away. She thought she perceived the rumor of light almost, as if from the corner of her eye, but whenever she turned to look, it was gone.

There were shadowy visions too – indistinct shapes flitted around her, clawing at her being with phantasmal, grasping fingers that dragged her down into evil dreams. The fog would seem to part a little from time to time, but just when she thought that she was about to stumble back into the light it once again enveloped her, ruthlessly drawing her back into darkness. The desire to cease her struggles was strong. She felt that if she but closed her eyes, surrendered to the groping, tugging shadows, and embraced the long and dreamless sleep that beckoned to her seductively, relief of all of her miseries could at long last be hers.

She was not sure at all what made her resist the temptation. Snow White did not know why she strove so hard - aimlessly wandering in the void, fighting the amorphous shadows away - except that she had a vague but persistent notion, that such an outcome was simply not right. As long and twisting as her tale had already been, she just could not accept it ending this way. There was more of her story left to tell. She just knew there was!

Snow White had no idea how long she languished in this purgatory of neither sleep nor wakefulness, somewhere between life and death, but as limitless as the void seemed in the moment, in less than a moment it simply ceased. It was almost as if she heard a great screaming and wailing in her ears that she had not previously noticed - an enormous cacophony of indistinct, tumultuous sound, that had gone on so long and so loud that she failed to recognize it for what it was any longer. It fell abruptly still as if cut off with a switch and the subsequent silence was deafening. Her tired, red-rimmed eyes cracked open, but at first she could tell little difference.

It was dark. That was Snow White's first thought – pitch dark, but it was a different sort of dark. It was *less* somehow. She would later find it impossible to explain the difference even to herself, but the best way she could express it was that the shadows before seemed great, malevolent pillars of dread tearing at her heart and soul, leaching her strength away. By comparison, the darkness she now perceived seemed a simple absence of light. It was almost reassuring, but that relief did not last.

The next sensation that she became aware of was pain. It was a throbbing, nagging, pulsing pain that seemed to afflict every nerve of her body. Even her hair ached. She recalled her desperate prayer back before the shadows took her and began to seriously reconsider her request to the Almighty.

Snow White felt something hard, bitter, and gritty filling her mouth. Weakly, she tried to spit it out, but found that she did not have the strength. She whimpered.

"Snowy!" exclaimed someone in broken relief. She thought it sounded like Erfreut, but could still see nothing. "Is she alright, sire? Will she…?"

"Sir! If you please!" chided a deep voice that she did not recognize in a stern whisper. "She must have absolute silence. And keep those curtains drawn! The light might bring the fits back. The danger has not yet passed – not by a long shot. Hand me another piece of charcoal."

Snow White felt fingers in her mouth. The hard gritty something was removed but quickly replaced and she moaned in protest. The princess felt a strong, gentle hand on her forehead.

"Be still, my lady," soothed the unfamiliar voice. "You must rest. Sleep now."

Snow White felt horrible. How could she possibly sleep? Did she even dare? She could not clearly remember the horrors of the sucking dark she had just escaped, but she feared them. She knew that they might still be there; lurking on the edges of her consciousness, just waiting for her to close her eyes to envelope her once more.

She tried to sit up, but could not so much as raise her head from her pillow. Every muscle ached. Her stomach was still twisted in painful, cramping knots and she felt infirmly weak. Something hard and cold was pushed beneath her hips and the hand on her forehead moved down to firmly press on her abdomen. Her bladder emptied and she whimpered again in pain and embarrassment. A tear escaped the corner of her eye.

"The charcoal will leach much of the poison out," said the voice softly in her ear, "but you must pass the rest. We've still a long ways to go. Dwarf," he commanded in a stern whisper, "bring me some more water."

"Yes, your Highness," replied Erfreut, who quickly rose to do as he was bidden.

"Who would do something so cruel to such a fair, young thing?" The voice murmured sadly. Snow White felt the strong, warm hand resume stroking her hair. "Who could possibly wish you ill? By God, you cannot die. If there is any justice in Heaven at all, you cannot. Live, princess, and I swear I will care for you. Live and you will want for nothing ever again…"

The gentle words calmed her. There was certain guilelessness in the voice – an inexplicable, hapless earnestness. Snow White could not explain why, but for the first time in many, many years and much to her own surprise, she felt that she could truly and implicitly trust this stranger. She wanted to believe him. It had been so long since she had anyone to take care of her…

Snow White's eyes began growing heavy again. So few words, but somehow the stranger beside her made her believe that everything really would be alright in the end. It stole the harshest sting from her pain.

"Rest now, princess," the voice soothed.

It said something more, but Snow White did not hear it. She was asleep.

*

When Snow White awoke again, it felt much more like the gentle transition from the land of dreams to the waking world with which she had long been familiar. The first thing she noticed was his eyes. They were a bright, piercing blue, shone with deep kindness, and peered at her fondly. The morning sun was brilliant at the man's back and made it appear as if his golden hair smoldered. She did not believe that she had ever seen another human being so beautiful.

"Am I dead?" She asked in a breathy croak, her voice all but inaudible. "Are you an angel?"

The beautiful, young man laughed. It was a warm, pleasant sound and immediately reassured her. He stroked her hair and gently cupped her cheek.

"No to both of your questions, princess," he replied. "Though I must say, it was a near thing. You gave us all quite a fright."

"Who are you?" she asked weakly. "How do you know who I am? What happened? I feel awful!"

"Of that I have no doubt," the young man answered seriously. "You very nearly died. Although, we were hoping that you could tell us how you found yourself in such a state.

"As to your other question," he went on, "I must confess that I have been a bit of a gossip during your repose. I fear that I might already know much that you might have wished to reveal to me yourself, but circumstance dictated a certain… loquaciousness, if you will. I do apologize, if you find I have pried too deeply. I am just glad that I was near enough to help. I am admittedly no healer, but have unfortunately seen more than a few poisonings in my time at court. I have never seen someone as stricken as you recover however. You must hail from hearty stock indeed!"

Snow White could not immediately reply. The sudden flood of fair speech left her head spinning

"As to who I am," he continued, clearing his throat auspiciously, unconsciously straightening in his seat at the foot of

Snow White's bed. "My name is Charming Von Gerechtigkeit Von Freide Von Gnadenbrot, Crowned Prince of Geschictia." The prince flashed a small, self-depreciating smile. "I promise that I am not as pompous as that sounds…"

"Of course not, Your Highness," Snow White replied quickly in a very small voice as she gazed up at his handsome face. She offered her own tiny smile. In spite of his denials, he still appeared inarguably angelic to her.

"How do you feel, princess?" he asked solicitously. "Is there any pain?"

"Yes," she answered truthfully. "I ache all over and I cannot move… My stomach…"

Just then, as if in response to her comment, her belly gurgled plaintively and her eyes opened wide in alarm.

"Oh!" cried Charming as he heard it too.

He quickly grabbed a nearby chamber pot and rolled the ailing princess to her side just in the nick of time. The uncontrollable bowel movement was accompanied by a ghastly sound and Snow White's face flushed beet crimson in the most acutely mortified degree of shame that she had ever known or had ever feared to know in her whole life before. When it passed, the prince wiped her off carefully with a damp towel and set the whole reeky mess on the other side of the room beside the door. Then he rearranged her bed clothes and patted the princess' head.

"I'm so, so sorry your Majesty!" Snow White gasped, humiliated tears streaming from the corners of her eyes.

She had never in her life wanted so fiercely to crawl away and die somewhere as she did right at that moment. She clenched her eyes tightly closed wishing passionately that she might disappear altogether.

"Shhh," shushed the prince. "Do not apologize. It is to be expected. You are still terribly ill."

He began to gently stroke her hair once more. Each firm pass of his warm hand made the shame seem a little less.

"Now," he continued tenderly. "I'm sure you will think me terribly presumptuous, but I must confess that I feel I've really gotten to know you quite well these past three days, my dear Snow White." He gave her an ironic smile and she could not help but weakly return it. "I pray, grant me a boon. It would please me very much if you would deem to dispense with all of the excessive panegyric of our respective stations and just call me Charming."

"Of… Of course, Charming," she murmured.

Something inside of her changed in that moment, she realized. She could not really define what that change was, but she suddenly saw the prince through new eyes. It was as if a small, stubborn door in her heart had been thrown wide and the first fresh breeze in ages swept all the staleness within away. How long had it been since someone actually cared how she felt? How long had it been since anyone has asked her opinion on anything or even addressed her as a person?

There came a tentative knock at the door and a hesitant head nervously peaked through as it opened a crack. Snow White smiled as she recognized the shy, blonde-bearded face.

"Erfreut!" She smiled happily in recognition.

"Ah yes," replied the prince with a grin. "How rude of me! I should have known that you would want to see your companions as soon as possible. They have been positively beside themselves with worry on your behalf." He turned to the door. "Yes, by all means you may come in…"

The dwarves practically tripped over themselves in their rush to push into the room. After offering profuse gratitude and thanks to the prince for all of his efforts, they quickly surrounded Snow White's bed. Profound relief shone in all of their faces.

Old, white-bearded Artz was the first to speak as was usual, though he cleared his throat several times before beginning. He opened his mouth, then shut it, then opened it again.

"We're glad to see you awake, child." He choked out at last, clearly overcome by powerful emotions. The others quickly murmured their agreement.

"Oh, Snowy…" Erfreut pushed his way forward and firmly grasped her hand. Tears streamed down his face, dampening his pink cheeks and shimmering in his thin, blonde beard like diamonds. "It's good to see you lass," he intoned passionately, squeezing her fingers even harder. "*Good* to see you!"

All of the others quickly followed suite, offering other brief, if intense expressions of relief. None of the blunt old dwarves seemed able to articulate what they felt very clearly, but the powerful emotion in the room was poignant. It actually surprised Snow White a little bit. For the most part, she felt that she had gotten along with the dwarves fairly well over the past few months that she dwelt with them. Her lot in life had certainly improved under their roof, but she had always understood their relationship as mostly business.

She cooked and cleaned for them – skills she had developed expertly back at Castle Wolfejager – and they allowed her a place to stay and food to eat. She had gotten along best with Erfreut, of course, and would almost consider him her friend, but the others had mostly ranged from politely courteous to coolly detached. She had actually been quite certain that Grantig did not like her at all, but it was actually he, standing wordlessly at the foot of her bed, who was most obvious in his weeping. The flood of emotion was actually a little overwhelming.

They did not stay long. Snow White was still extremely weak and weary from her ordeal and tired quickly. The dwarves, for their part, found they had little to say anyway and after another round of profound expressions of relief at her recovery, they slowly filed out. Erfreut set a little white flower on her pillow as he left last of all.

"You are fortunate to have subjects so loyal," noted the prince as the door clicked shut. He picked up the flower, sniffed it, and then set it prettily behind Snow White's ear. "It is clear that they love you well."

Snow White turned her eyes to the sealed portal fondly.

"Yes, Charming, I am fortunate," she replied with a small sigh. She fluffed the flower Charming had placed in her hair before meeting his gaze sincerely. "Very fortunate, but I rule over no one. They are not my subjects. They are my dear friends." As she said the words she realized for the first time that they were true. "I am very lucky to have met them. They were more kind to me than I had any right to demand or expect…"

Charming nodded sagely.

They talked long after that and often over the next few days. As guarded as Snow White had ever been with most other people, it was easy to talk to the prince. There was just something incredibly magnetic and disarming about him. She found herself divulging details of her life and long mistreatment that she had never shared with anyone before.

The whole time, Charming listened attentively, occasionally making some sympathetic comment or asking a concerned question. He remained calm and pleasant, offering many a sweet smile that stole the young princess' breath, but it was obvious that a fire kindled behind his blue eyes every time she spoke of her abuse at the hands of Arglist. It was only an expression, a slight twist to his fine facial features, but it was the first time Snow White had seen anyone react to her stepmother with anything but fear. It charmed and fascinated her. Could this man really be so strong?

One morning, about a week and a half after the day she had awakened, she was at last strong enough to sit up in her bed by herself. As had become their custom, Snow White talked and the prince listened until long after the bright morning sunlight shining through the window had faded to afternoon shadows. Just before dusk, she finished telling all there was to tell. Charming looked resolute and grim, but Snow White felt as if her soul had been unburdened. It was as if a great weight had been lifted from her heart.

"What you tell me of this Arglist is appalling," stated the prince darkly. He practically spat her step mother's name as if it was distasteful to him. Courtesy had dictated he hold his peace until the princess finished speaking hers, but he did not feel constrained any longer. "Any one of the horrors you describe would constitute high treason in my own country. No beast, nor peasant, nor even highwayman or heathen deserves to be treated so shabbily. By God, I will not abide it!"

Charming stood and began pacing. "That some low-born pretender should be allowed to defy the very order of the Almighty and commit such trespass against her betters unchallenged is intolerable!" His words were impassioned but still he did not raise his voice.

Snow White sighed.

"Prince Charming," she said. "Your words are kind and your sympathy much appreciated. I thank you, but what am I to do? I have no armies to command. I have no supporters among my father's nobles to rally to my cause. I don't even really know any of them that well. It might be best if I could simply disappear and escape her all together. I'm sure she thinks me dead. In fact, I'm still not exactly certain about that myself..."

"I understand your fear, princess," stated Charming firmly. "But such a vile thing cannot be allowed to remain unpunished. I would find a harsh judgment before my God indeed, if I allowed such heterodoxy to fester unchecked. Royal blood is not so generously bestowed upon humanity. Where such refinement is allowed to be diminished by the banal, we shall only find darkness and judgment in its wake. We both have a duty to right this foul injustice – yours to defend from this usurper what has been bestowed upon you by birth and providence, and mine to protect the very order of God by which I myself will one day rule. It cannot be otherwise. Providence has surely put me in your path, Snow White. It is destiny that we have met!"

Charming's eyes widened suddenly, as if he had just realized something that should have been long obvious. He became very intense.

"Yes," he murmured, falling to one knee and taking Snow White's small white hand in his own. He stared deeply into her mahogany brown eyes. "It is destiny. I see that now. It was God who had me ranging so far afield in an unfamiliar wilderness. It was He who brought your little friend so swiftly to my side in your hour of need. And it is He who has spared your life. It cannot be mere chance that all of this has happened.

"You are so very good and gentle, Snow White," he whispered. "You are so very beautiful. That I should go hunting boar, but instead discover so fair a princess alone and unprotected in the trackless wilds… It cannot be mere chance! I cannot deny such a clear message placed directly before me in my path. God has brought you to me, Snow White. It must be His will that we set things aright. It must be His will that we be together!"

Snow White found her heart beating very quickly. The prince's hand was warm and strong. His face was so very handsome. She was not at all displeased by what she was hearing, but at the same time could think of nothing intelligent to offer in reply.

"I will be your protector, Snow White," Charming declared. "If you will have me, I will take you as my own and cherish you all of your days. Come with me and be my wife!"

A very small voice inside her head told her that this was preposterous. One simply did not go off marrying strangers they had just met after only a few days and one long conversation, prince or not. However, Snow White told the voice to be quiet. She found that she could not argue with Charming's impassioned words. She did not even really want to. In fact, nothing had ever seemed so obvious and clear.

Her heart was soaring. It felt as if something she had been searching for ever since her father died was suddenly right at hand for the taking. This man was powerful. He was beautiful. He had just saved her life and helped her unburden her very soul. Here was someone who would finally care for her and end all of her miserable years of loneliness and solitude. How could she refuse?

"It must be so," murmured the princess intensely. "It *must* be so. How could I choose otherwise?"

Then Charming embraced her. His lips swiftly found hers. Snow White had never kissed a man before and was initially caught off guard, but did not resist. The prince's mouth was soft and warm against hers. The sensation of it stirred her heart within her breast and she returned his embrace fiercely.

When Charming finally released her he said, "As soon as you are recovered, princess, we shall return you to your lands and people and herald your triumphant homecoming every step of the way!"

"What do you mean, Charming?" Snow White asked in puzzlement.

"To take back your kingdom," he explained. "All we will need is a wedding..."

"I'm sorry Charming," Snow White shook her head in confusion." I don't understand at all what you mean."

"This woman has tried to murder you once by proxy and thrice by her own hand," Charming stated. "We shall plan our wedding with all the majesty and grandeur at my disposal. Our wedding procession shall announce the tidings of our engagement all the way to the very gates of Castle Wolfejager. We shall invite all of the gentry sworn to your father and then I shall strike my pavilion within shouting distance of the walls!" he finished grandly. He gave a quick feral smile. "We shall invite The Queen Regent Arglist to join us as well."

"What?!" exclaimed the Princess. "To what possible end?!"

"So that she might face justice, my princess," Charming replied gently. "So that you might start in our marriage free from fear. Though she clearly has no respect or regard for royal command, her own obsession will force her to attend. She will not be able to stay away.

"Even if she is... reluctant, let's say, to accept our invitation," the prince went on. "She will have little choice. We shall insist she attend. Then we shall have her. You are the lawful ruler and heir of Gutefehia. She is a faithless pretender and the thugs and miscreants who attend her will quickly abandon her in the face of righteous judgment! She shall face justice in answer for the pain she has caused you..."

Snow White was unconvinced, but Charming was insistent. They did just as he proposed and as everyone knows now, he was proven right.

Chapter 7

Snow White was on her hands and knees. Light streamed in through the open window, reflecting off of the millions of dust motes suspended in the air to brilliant effect. It looked almost like a spotlight from on high shone directly down onto the queen. A few more of the pigeons she had disturbed earlier had returned to their perches. Though they regarded this intruding human suspiciously, they continued to coo softly in their nests.

The queen was feeling very confused. She still detected the acute wrenching pain in her stomach, but recollections of those first few nearly miraculous days with Charming left her feeling almost giddy with pleasure. She shook her head to clear it and again looked up at the mirror.

"Certainly, Mirror," she began when she at last regained her composure. "Certainly I was lucky, but it was all Charming. He saved me. What did I do, but nearly get myself murdered! Without him…"

She gasped and her heart skipped a beat as the image in the mirror once again changed. He seemed so suddenly vivid in her mind. Could it really be him? Golden hair, piercing blue eyes, firm youthful skin, and dressed in full ceremonial regalia - her Charming was as handsome as the first day she laid eyes upon him so many years ago.

It had been such a weird, improbable encounter. In so many ways, that day had been both the very best and very worst of her life. How had so many impossible circumstances aligned that cool October afternoon to save her life and lead to her long, blissful marriage?

Her eyes filled with tears as she gazed at her husband's beautiful, tranquil face in the looking glass. She was not at all certain if they were tears of joy at seeing him again so unexpectedly or grief for his absence. Her fingers brushed the hard, cold surface of the mirror. What she would not give to be able to touch his skin once more. How she missed that face! So close and yet so distant. She was forced to look away

Out of the blue he had swooped down, picked her up, and carried her away from the agony of her previous life. He had slain her demons and shown her love for the very first time. Despite how broken he had found her, Charming had been so tender and patient. Snow White stared hard at her husband in the mirror until she felt the now familiar falling sensation again, but this time it was a soft landing.

***

Charming pushed the heavy door open with his foot. The fire was already roaring in the grate. The bed was freshly made with fluffy down quilts, warm woolen blankets and soft satin sheets. A fresh bottle of fine, mulled wine sat on the bedside table along with two glasses.

The prince carried his new bride across the threshold of their bed chamber and tried to kiss her, but the bulky white fabric, of Snow White's fabulous wedding dress kept getting in his mouth. He growled playfully and pitched her onto the bed making her squeal. Then he leapt up to lie beside her. They both laughed until their sides hurt.

It had been a marvelous ceremony. Charming spared no expense. A veritable army of Geschictian laborers and servants made Snow White's long neglected palace virtually radiate with immaculacy and splendor.

Decades of dust and cobwebs were cleared. Stable hands worked madly to shovel away years of decomposing excrement from the stables. Royal game keepers supervised big eared chausies as they slunk their stealthy feline ways into every nook and cranny of Castle Wolfejager, wreaking a veritable catastrophe of fear and destruction upon the legions of rats and mice that apparently indwelt every darkened corner.

The long disused chapel had been blanketed in white and blue silks and extravagantly crammed to bursting with fresh flowers even though it was well autumn. Lilac scented candles stood at regular intervals upon sterling silver candelabras transforming the stale, stagnant odor of moldering disuse that Snow White always remembered into the pleasant aroma of springtime.

An artful chamber quintet played and a masterful choir beautifully sang the processional and recessional. Charming had also presented his princess with an honor guard of her own House soldiers gleaming and resplendent in brand new, polished silver mail and spotless white livery. The ceremony had been beautiful and the feasting afterward excessive and joyous. The princess could not have dreamt it any better.

When their giggles finally subsided, Charming tenderly brushed away a strand of inky black hair from Snow White's radiantly glowing face with the back of his hand.

"We're finally alone, my love," he breathed into her ear then kissed her cheek and neck. "I was beginning to think our guests would never let me have you!"

Snow White giggled, but then sighed and gazed deeply into Charming's piercing blue eyes. "Well, I'm all yours now, my husband." She laughed again, but found that once begun, she could not easily stop.

Charming looked at her. "What, Snow White? What is it? What's so funny?" He asked with a bemused smile

"I have a *husband*!" She hugged him and beamed even more brilliantly. The gesture pleasantly dimpled her soft, pale cheeks.

"Oh! I never thought this day would come, Charming," she breathed. "And it has been everything I could have dreamt of... And more! I thought for so long I would always be alone. I never believed that anyone could love me after my father died. I thought I was doomed to misery and pain forever, until you came. I never thought I could escape Arglist's..."

"Shhh," he shushed her, laying a gentle finger against her lips. "Let us make no further mention of that woman here. That issue is settled. All is well now and ever will be. I promise you that. In fact..." He sat up straighter and puffed out his chest in extremely exaggerated fashion.

"I hereby decree!" He began officiously. "That henceforth and ever after, there shall never again be another hurtful thought or harsh word spoken in this room!" He met her eyes seriously then and murmured, "In a world of scheming, petty nobles, backbiting, politics, and strife, this shall be our sanctuary – a private little world that is just yours and mine."

Snow White smiled and he kissed her deeply. Then he began undoing the buttons on his shirt.

"And like any other good sanctuary," he whispered into her ear with a wicked grin. "All it needs now is to be properly sanctified." Charming nibbled on her earlobe and his big hand moved to gently cup her breast.

He was quite a bit older than her - she would turn seventeen in just over a month, and he was nearly thirty - but Snow White actually liked that about him. He was steady - always seeming to know just what to do. He made her feel safe. Also, Snow White could not deny how handsome she found him. His chest was broad and well-muscled and his hands felt strong but gentle, even through the thick material of her voluminous wedding gown. Still, the princess began to tremble. His touch startled her.

She had never seen so much as a man's bared ankle before! Now her beautiful husband lay beside her shirtless, touching her as no one had ever touched her, kissing her as she had never been kissed. It was confusing.

His closeness suddenly made her feel both extremely uncomfortable as well as undeniably enticed. The contradiction of emotions made her stomach twist and turn. Charming's soft lips moved from her ear to her neck and she sucked in a sudden breath of alarm as he softly bit her flesh. It did not really hurt. In fact, she would almost call the sensation pleasant, but it was nothing at all she had expected.

She swallowed hard. Snow White's breath was beginning to come in short gasps as Charming's hand slipped unobtrusively under her dress to slide slowly up her bare calf and thigh. When his thick fingers began to gently caress the soft tissue beneath her small clothes, she jumped.

The princess willed her voice to be steady, but it still came out as a frightened squeak. "Ma... My... Hu... Husband!" She whispered breathlessly. "Wha... What..." She gulped. "What are you going to do?"

The princess immediately flushed crimson, hating how much like a frightened little girl she sounded. She was a woman and a wife for goodness sake! She would be queen of two nations one day! She could not deny it, however. Though she certainly wanted to please her new husband, she had prepared herself for none of what was happening now. Snow White was scared.

Charming looked up in puzzlement. "What is it, Dearest?" He asked innocently. "What's the..." He trailed off as he caught site of her clearly frightened face.

She was briefly afraid that he would be angry with her, but the prince grinned instead. Snow White was surprised by the sudden, impulsive notion that she would have almost welcomed a rage instead. She felt her cheeks grow hot and hid her face in her hands, feeling a total fool.

"Oh," he said, shaking his head at his own thickness. "I understand. I..." He licked his lips and trailed off as he considered how best to proceed. "I don't suppose," he began again at last. "I don't suppose your mother... that is, your real mother, ever talked with you about... men and women... love?"

Snow White squeezed her eyes tightly shut - feeling humiliated by her unconscionable ignorance. She shook her head silently.

The prince nodded.

"No one has talked about it with..." Charming again trailed off as his young princess shook her head once more vigorously 'no'. He sighed deeply and sat up. "I see."

He got up from the bed and Snow White suddenly wanted nothing else so fiercely as to crawl up under a rock and die of shame. She was ruining her own wedding night! The princess started to cry.

"I... I'm... so... sorry!" She sobbed. "It's just... I haven't... I've never... seen a man, like this before! I've never been touched like... Please don't be angry with me! I..."

Charming gently took her by the hand and coaxed her to stand.

"It's alright," he said. He kissed her lightly on the cheek and looked deeply into her eyes. "This is our night. Be at ease. I don't want you to be upset. I would that afterwards you remember tonight fondly with naught but joy. I will not press you into anything you find too uncomfortable, but let me ask you this, Snow White, if I may. Do you love me?"

"Of... Of course, Charming! I..."

"Do you believe that I love you?"

"Certainly I do..!

"Do you think I would ever hurt you?" He patiently continued.

"No!" exclaimed the princess. "No, of course not! I..."

"Do you trust me?" he pressed softly.

Snow White was silent for a moment. What they were doing made her feel awkward certainly, but Charming would not force her into anything unseemly, she felt. She did not believe that he would deceive her into doing anything that was not perfectly right and proper.

"Yes, of course I do," she murmured sincerely. "I trust you with my life! With... with my... my everything!"

Then trust me now." He smiled. "Relax, Dearest One. You are my wife who I have sworn this day before God and Man to cherish and protect always. Give yourself to me. *Entrust* yourself to me, and I will treat you as gently as a baby bird in my palm. It is no shame not to know that which you have not been taught. Trust me to teach you, my princess."

Snow White did not immediately stop crying, but did feel less uneasy. She tentatively laid her head against her husband's bare chest and embraced him, getting used to the warmth of his bare skin against hers, his musky smell. When she finally calmed herself enough to think intelligently again, she realized that she liked it. Snow White squeezed Charming firmly and met his eyes at last.

"I will," she promised intensely. "I will trust you. Teach me how to be a wife."

"Then let us say no more." He kissed her.

The prince's hands slid up her back to undo the clasps holding the bodice of her dress closed. They were extremely tight and came free only with a great deal of fumbling and tugging that made them both giggle. The laughter seemed to leach away the last of Snow White's reticence.

When the last clasp came free, the billowing, white garment cascaded down around her ankles and Charming pulled her to him. The shirtless prince tugged the stubborn knot in the laces holding Snow White's corset in place. When at last it unraveled, the tight bindings of the constricting garment retreated like frightened snakes and Snow White was able to take her first deep breath in hours. Charming put both of his big hands on her bare shoulders and took a moment to gaze upon his stunning, young bride.

Snow White's large, dark eyes looked up at the prince intensely, expectantly, high cheekbones tinged shyly pink. She was not sure what was coming exactly, but was now resolved to embrace it, and her small, pert breasts rose and fell visibly in nervous anticipation.

She was quite a small woman, but her body was tight, healthy and nicely shaped. Perhaps as a consequence of her long forced labor, her stomach was flat - muscles taught and well-defined through alabaster skin. Her short, sable hair was so dark it nearly looked blue and framed her pale face beautifully.

Snow White was acutely conscious of the fact that she was now completely naked. Despite the roaring fire, the large room was still a little chilly and her nipples perked erectly. The stark contrast of Charming's warm hands on her shoulders was actually very pleasant, but her heart was beating at frightful pace. She met his kind blue eyes unwaveringly, determined not to recoil again.

His hands slid slowly down from her narrow shoulders to briefly caress her breasts before continuing their descent to gently cup her tiny bottom. He pulled her close and as she first felt her bare skin press against his hard chest Snow White felt something stir within her. It was a pleasant, warm moistness that slowly grew between her legs and a strange, inexplicable longing in her heart for even greater closeness still. It was something akin to hunger – a sudden desire to fulfill, a craving that she had never known she had before. She did not completely understand it, but felt a sudden, fervent desire to surrender to it.

Charming's grip on her backside tightened. He lifted her from the floor and their lips met in a passionate kiss – the princes' tongue eagerly exploring the inside of her mouth. It seemed the most natural thing in the world to wrap her arms and legs tightly around his body.

He carried her to the bed once more and laid her upon it, pausing only to untie his trousers. He slowly descended on top of her, hungrily kissing her mouth, then her neck, then her breasts. Again his big fingers found their way to her soft, secret parts and Snow White moaned in contentment as he gently began to caress her. As he rubbed her, his mouth slid down, first to kiss her flat, tight stomach, then to join his wandering hand. Snow White felt his tongue venture inside of her.

The feelings flooding her senses were the strongest she'd ever experienced before. Simultaneous sensations of indescribable pleasure, unquenchable desire and immeasurable love filled her. Emotions so intense demanded some form of verbal expression and as the pleasure between her legs intensified through the eager ministrations of Charming's nimble tongue, she cried out.

"I trust you, I trust you, I trust you…" she moaned breathily over and over again.

Snow White felt something hot and hard against her right foot. Charming took his time, but his lips gradually rose from between her legs, back up to her stomach, then again to her breasts and nipples. His right hand continued to rub between Snow White's thighs. She felt the hard, hot something rub against her leg, then press against the thin, moist hair between her legs. Her heart was beating at an impossible pace, thundering in her ears and her breathing was labored. Charming looked easily just as impassioned and again their eyes met. He hesitated.

"I trust you," the princess whispered intensely. "I *trust* you!" She felt a firm, steady pressure and her eyes opened wide as she realized that her husband was slowly pushing inside of her. She looked down and saw his engorged penis steadily disappearing into her body.

"I trust you. I trust you, Charming. I trust you…" She repeated over and over again. The pressure between her legs increased. It felt undeniably strange, but also perfectly right and good – as if her prince had been specifically made to fit this spot within her just exactly.

There was a firm, final thrust, a sudden pop, and a flash of pain as Charming entered her fully. She screamed and held onto him more tightly, digging her long, meticulously painted nails deep into his back.

"Inside me!" she gasped. "Oh, God! I feel you inside me! Oh! Charming! I feel… I… feel…"

She could not finish saying what it was she felt. The prince was penetrating her deeply. Each thrust came in rapid succession and stole her thoughts. She wrapped her legs tightly around his waist as his hips continued to vigorously pound against hers.

The powerful feelings of pleasure grew in intensity until she thought they must surely burst from her body. Snow White cried louder and louder with each additional thrust until she could bear it no longer. She screamed, arching her back, pressing her throbbing pelvis against her husband's loins just as he called out the same. She felt him pulsing inside of her and Charming seemed to go boneless. He collapsed across her body. They both lay there for a long moment, motionless but for their labored breathing. Then desperately, Snow White's lips sought his.

This time it was Snow White's tongue that was eager. This time it was she who fiercely grasped her husband close, greedily demanding more kisses. It felt as though Charming had just revealed the greatest most glorious secret in the whole of creation and it was she alone upon whom he had decided to bestow it. She clutched him against her desperately, never wanting this closeness to end even as he went flaccid, slowly shrinking out of her along with a hot flood of semen, blood, and her own passionate juices.

She met his gaze fiercely - nearly unable to speak, certainly unable to express all she felt at that moment.

"I do trust you Charming," she murmured. "I will always trust you!" Then she pulled him close again, burying his face in her breasts and kissing his head over and over. "Always, my prince. Always!"

"Yes, my princess," Charming swore fervently. "Forever and always…"

Chapter 8

"That's the end of the story then, I suppose."

The harsh droning of the mirrors voice called Snow White abruptly out of her blissful reverie. She still had a euphoric, warm tingle permeating all throughout her being, and a pleasant flush to her cheeks, but quickly turned her face to the magic looking glass in irritation.

"What do you mean, 'the end of the story'?" she demanded sternly. "It was the ending of a great deal of pain certainly, but it was the beginning of a wonderful life with the most wonderful man I have ever known! A life that is over now…" she trailed off sadly.

"But really! That was it?" The mirror continued insistently. "You married the prince then hi-ho, happily ever after! No problems ever again?"

"I don't understand what it is you are asking…"

"Do not forget that I see you inside and out – all the way through!" The mirror scoffed. "You can lie to yourself, but let me assure you, Your Majesty, you cannot lie to me!"

"Lie to..? How Dare..! Why are you trying to anger me?" The queen exclaimed. "I loved my husband! I would not trade an instant of the life we had together. Everything was perfect! Everything *was* perfect…" she murmured then trailed off into sullen silence again. Charming had always known just what to do, just how to put everything to rights. She missed his steadying assurance. No matter what happened she had always known that Charming could make everything come out fine in the end. She smiled slightly at the thought and made the looking glass swirl.

"Charming always knew just how to fix things…" She sighed then stared back into the mirror, eagerly this time.

***

"I will thank you both to comport yourselves appropriately in the royal presence." Charming's deep, placid voice did not rise as he addressed the bickering lords. He never raised his voice. That was something that the young princess loved about him. He was as patient as a saint with a temper as even and calm as a mountain pool.

Still, the softly spoken words cut the two arguing men off as abruptly as if a hand had been clapped over their mouths.

"His Royal Majesty King Justice, my Lord Father, is ill," Charming continued sternly. "He is old and the journey from Geschictia was burdensome for him. He is in repose presently and does not need his sleep disturbed by such a raucous, boorish display. Have a thought for your dignity! I am quite sure that your shouting can be heard beyond the castle walls and well off into the countryside besides! You shall both have your say, if you can control your emotions, but if not," his eyes narrowed. "It would pain me to have you escorted to the dungeon to regain your composure. I trust I shall not have to mention it again."

Count Bemessen and Lord Stolz both looked at their feet and mumbled hasty apologies.

"Now," Charming stated firmly. "Lord Stolz, please explain your grievance with Count Bemessen."

"Yes, your Highness..."

Lord Stolz was the Earl of Schweinefett, a prosperous fief that neighbored both the direct holdings of the King of Geschictia as well as the sea. As a consequence, he was a fabulously rich, immensely fat man. In fact, the prodigious size of his body was surpassed only by the enormity of his overinflated opinion of himself and his own importance.

Snow White did not know him well, (he was a member of King Justice's Court, not her own), but could not help thinking he looked a bit like a painted clown today. His face was heavily caked with white make-up and there was a tiny, faux mole painted on at the corner of his mouth. He also wore an impressive powdered wig, which stood atop his head like a tower that a band of rebellious sheep might have constructed to ward off invasion. Every inch of the rest of his bulbous body was cocooned in a blinding array of bright colors, heavy embroidery and a veritable explosion of filigreed silk, satin, and lace. The young princess doubted that she herself had half that much fabric in her entire wardrobe.

"This beslubbering, dog-hearted, fustilarian..." Stolz began pompously thrusting an accusatory finger at Bemessen.

"My Lord," the prince interrupted simply, but there was enough warning in his eyes to bring the blustering earl to a halt. His jowly cheeks flushed brilliantly pink in embarrassment.

"My deepest apologies, Highness," he murmured contritely with a low bow before spluttering on in a tightly constricted voice. "But this... this... this *person*, has caused me mortal insult. I will not abide it! I demand redress!"

"Go on," instructed Charming evenly. "What did he do?" Stolz flushed even more deeply pink. "This... This mammering mammet dared to flaunt his churlish vulgarities in the presence of his betters! With no regard whatsoever for my station, he impudently refused to remove his horses to the rear stalls in the stables so that my men might more conveniently quarter mine. Clearly, proper etiquette, which he as a foreigner is obviously nescient of, dictates that as host he should have immediately surrendered the space to the guesting gentry of Geschictia as a simple matter of hospitality. That is then to say nothing of defying one of superior pedigree!

"Not only did he flatly refuse this right and completely reasonable request," Stolz blustered on. "But he dared to address me vilely – casting positively libelous aspersions upon my House - and even went so far as to calumniate no one other than my dear and sainted mother! Finally, he crowned this philistine display by daring to bare his rank, pox-marked, hairy *bottom* in my presence!"

Snow White could not completely cover her reflexive snort of laughter, though she quickly covered her mouth with her hand. The lapse embarrassed her, but Charming shot her a sideways glance and a tiny smile that made her feel immediately better. This public expression of the princess' amusement seemed to represent permission to the other members of the court however, and a low murmur of chuckling ran through the crowd. There was no mistaking that the nobles who hailed from Snow White's court in Gutefehia laughed loudest.

The laughter only served to infuriate the foppish lord more thoroughly. His fat, pink face darkened to near purple.

"Am I to be humiliated before all the court?!" Stolz bellowed. "Shall I endure insult from this artless, base-court, apple-john?! I demand satisfaction! What do you intend to do about this, your Highness?! The very dignity of our nation has been unpardonably shamed! My good name is besmirched!"

Charming did an admirable job of hiding most of his annoyance. These sorts of silly disputes were all too common as he and his new wife tried to knit their two kingdoms together. He turned his cold blue eyes to Count Bemessen.

Bemessen was nearly the exact opposite of Lord Stolz. Especially compared to the foppish earl, he was largely unadorned. He was also swarthy and rugged looking – tall and wiry. His long black hair was neatly pulled back into a simple ponytail revealing a stoic face that was not exactly ugly, but also nothing to arrest one's attention for any length of time either. In fact, had he been dressed differently, Snow White might have thought him a soldier, blacksmith or day laborer. His clothes were all of a very fine military cut, but dyed in subdued shades of brown, green, and black – still dapper, but not pretentious in the least.

"Well, my lord," the prince stated sternly. "Do you deny it? Is what Lord Stolz accuses you of true?"

"Every word of it, your Highness!" Bemessen replied loudly in a very pronounced burr.

He puffed out his chest proudly. This immediately elicited more raucous laughter from the Gutefehian contingent and, of course, also mightily infuriated the Geschictians. Soon the room roared with a tumult of angry voices.

Charming rolled his eyes in visible exasperation.

"Silence!" he hissed and the room became immediately still. "Regrettably, my Lords, I myself am but a guest in this Hall and would not presume upon the hospitality of our esteemed hostess." He turned to his wife. "What would you have me do, my love?" he asked pointedly.

"My... My Lord?" stuttered the young princess in surprise, but recovered quickly. "I... I would not presume to command you as our honored guest, Husband." She lilted pleasantly. "My only desire is for your utmost comfort and that of all who have accompanied you. In the interest of hospitality, I of course, trust your judgment to equitably resolve this matter."

Lord Bemessen's face fell, and he shot his future queen a look of utter, stark betrayal. At the same time Lord Stolz beamed in smug satisfaction.

"Very well," replied Charming. He turned to the fat earl. "Lord Stolz," he began.

"Yes, my liege!" Stolz replied quickly, his flabby face shining with victory.

"You say you have been insulted by this man?" the prince asked.

"In your very presence, my liege!" he answered.

"And you say you cannot bare the insult?" Charming continued.

"By God's teeth, I could not tarnish the good name of House Stolz so," he replied.

"And you require satisfaction?" questioned the prince again.

"My honor demands it, sire!"

"I see," Charming turned to Count Bemessen, who had gone a very greenish shade of pale. "Count Bemessen, Lord Stolz demands satisfaction for your admitted affront. Therefore, I shall allow him to obtain redress from you. You shall endure trial by combat... Should you deem to accept Lord Stolz challenge, of course.

"Since Lord Stolz is the challenger in this duel," Charming continued with a pointed glance at the portly earl. "You, Count Bemessen, may choose the weapon. What say you?"

It was almost as if the two squabbling gentry traded expressions. A slow smile spread across Bemessen's face at the same time that all the blood drained from that of Lord Stolz's. In fact, the flabbergasted earl looked as if he might faint dead away.

"Verily, I accept your Highness' most fair and equitable offer, Sire!" cried the count as he shot Stolz a triumphant grin. Then his eyes narrowed. "I select trial by two-handed broadsword!"

The Earl of Schweinefett took a staggering step backwards, much as if someone had struck him a physical blow. It was doubtful that the paunchy fop could even lift the heavy weapon.

"My... my... my... My Liege!" he stammered helplessly.

"You shall, of course, both select a Second tonight," Charming continued neutrally, pointedly ignoring the fat lord. "Whoever you choose will be in charge of making certain arrangements, should you fall in combat. These will include organizing the funeral, notifying next of kin, and cleaning up any mess left behind – you know, mopping up all the blood or other undesirable bodily fluids, collecting any dismembered bits that might remain, etc. etc... then rendering proper disposal. We shall reconvene the court here at dawn to witness that justice be served! Unless..." He trailed off.

"Unless what, my prince?" Stolz breathed in a very tiny voice.

"Unless, my good earl," stated Charming, leaning forward in his chair and folding his hands in front of him. "You can find it in your heart to forgive Count Bemessen and graciously allow him to keep his horses where they are as a gesture of cousinly good will and gratitude for the hospitality already provided."

"Um, uh, yes, my liege! Of course, my liege!" Stolz cried in obvious, almost comical relief, throwing up his hands as if offering exaltation to the Almighty. He nodded vigorously. "Perhaps, I spoke a bit too hastily. After all, graciousness is among the most noble of virtues and I would be happy to overlook this one, small misunderstanding, just this once. Count Bemessen is an honored cousin and host after all!"

"I'm sure we all admire your beneficence, my lord," Charming answered sardonically. "Then I trust the matter is resolved?"

"Y... Ye... Yes, my prince" stammered Stolz.

"And Count Bemessen?"

"Already forgotten, Highness," he answered quickly, new respect for this foreign prince vivid in his dark eyes.

"Very good then," replied Charming before addressing the entire assemblage. "I am weary. There will be no further audiences today. I look forward to seeing all of you on the marrow."

The assembled gentry quickly filed out of the throne room. When all of the nobles had gone, the prince also sent the guards away as well. He and his princess were left alone together.

Charming slouched back in his chair with a great, exasperated sigh. "By God's own wounds, I'm sick of this bickering!" he groaned and rubbed at his eyes. "I know this is Der Vaterland, but I am exceptionally tired of being Der Vater. Holding court with this lot is like marming a crowd of naughty children!"

Snow White put a gentle hand on his thigh and smiled.

"You handled it brilliantly though," she murmured. "At the risk of sounding horribly gouache, I think the Earl of Schweinefett, might have to change his trousers when he gets back to his own chambers!" She giggled girlishly, but then stuck her tongue out in disgust. "In fact, you did so well that I might let you handle it all by yourself next time. I *hate* sitting at audience!"

"Come near me, my lady wife," Charming commanded with a good-natured grin. She complied and he pulled her down to sit on his lap. His wandering hand found its way under her dress and up the bare skin of her leg. "As do I, but you know that we both must attend. You are still Crowned Princess of Gutefehia and I am still the

Crowned Prince of Geschictia. When we have a child, then our countries will be truly united and some of this nonsense might end…" He situated her to face him, his other hand joining the first under her dress. He kissed her again.

Snow White smiled down at Charming with a mischievous smirk.

"My Good Prince," she murmured silkily, "What are your intentions?"

Charming kissed his princess deeply

"You know, Snow White" he answered with a devilish grin. "The sooner we have a baby, the sooner we can slog all of this nonsense off on him."

Snow White closed her eyes and sighed contentedly as her husband began to urgently caress her body beneath her clothes. She could not agree more.

Chapter 9

"Is that so?" asked the mirror dubiously.

The harsh tone of the question shook Snow White out of her fond recollections. She scowled at the mirror.

"Is what so?" she rejoined testily.

"So your prince solved all of your problems for you?" it pressed. "You did nothing at all but lay about basking in the ephemeral glow of his noble presence for all of those years together? If I might respectfully disagree, that is utter *nonsense*. Would you care to look again?"

"To what purpose?" asked the queen, looking away in irritation. "I remember well enough! I was there after all. This is a waste of time. I'm going to go."

"Really?" scoffed the mirror. "Go and do what? Isn't the very reason you found your way up here to this lonely, filthy room in the first place because you had no idea where to go or what you should do? Have you achieved such clarity in the intervening time that all is set to rights now? Are you sure you would not like to look again?"

"There are no 'rights' anymore," mumbled Snow White sadly. The euphoria of her previous experience in the mirror faded and her all too familiar morose feelings were returning. Her lower lip began to quiver and tears formed at the corners of her eyes. "Not without him... Nothing will ever be right again! You don't know what it is like to be so alone..."

Snow White gazed longingly at the image of her husband in the mirror's shimmering depths. She knew that it could not really be him. The queen had stood by the tomb of his fathers as they laid his body in place and sealed the mausoleum doors shut. Yet, there he was before her, as youthful and dashing as ever he had been, but even farther out of her reach – nothing more than the shadow of a memory.

He regarded his queen sadly from the looking glass and Snow White sighed. This phantom of his past self was almost worse than his absence. Rather than uplift her, all his image seemed to do now was emphasize the magnitude of her loss. Without him all she felt was emptiness. Ever since that terrible day, nothing seemed right anymore. She looked down...

Snow White stared at her lap. The sable black velvet of the long, mourning gown gave stark contrast to the star-shaped, white blossoms of the bouquet lying there. They had been quite beautiful when Lady Anja had given them to her. Now they were faded and dry - a desiccated recollection of life and beauty that was no more - not unlike she herself, she thought.

She sat upon a heavy wooden chair in her bed chamber facing the cold, dead hearth. Her breath frosted in the February chill, but she did not really notice. In fact, had her ladies-in-waiting not nagged her so much about the cold and the importance of minding her health that she sent them all away, she probably would not have thought twice about it. Perhaps she secretly longed for the worst of their dire warnings to come to pass. Anything would have been better than the brokenhearted anguish she experienced now.

The queen did not know how long she sat there just staring at the withered bouquet, but it must have been quite some time. It was long enough that the small fire Anja had insisted on starting before she left was well extinguished, any residual traces of warmth long fled. It must have been hours ago, but still she felt no desire to do anything but stay right where she was. Snow White continued staring dumbly at the bundle of dead Lion's Foot on her lap, as if some great secret to the relief of her pain might be hidden therein.

Her eyes were red and burning and her dark, black eye make-up was streaked all over her face from crying. Her dress was still grungy and soiled at the knees from where she had collapsed in a weeping heap at the sealed mausoleum doors. Though she stared at them, she did not really see the flowers anymore. Instead, in her mind's eye, she saw only his beautiful face, nearly as familiar as her own – strong cheek bones, high, proud brow, thick silver hair and eyes closed as if merely sleeping, but pale, oh so very pale.

It had been surreal really. The whole time she sat next to his body at the funeral, she could not completely squelch the idea that all she need do to set the world right once more was simply reach out her hand and shake him, just as she had done so many countless mornings in the bed they shared. Then his striking blue eyes would open and he would look adoringly upon her once again. Even later, there in the royal crypts, with him lying motionless beside her upon the mensa, nothing felt amiss. Everything was as it should be, because he was with her.

Everyone had been appropriately somber, but among the murmurings of the so-called mourners, she could pick up on snatches of conversations, poorly framed questions that starkly revealed the abundance of thinly veiled narcissism. It was clear to her that most of those in attendance were only concerned about how the death of the king might impact them personally and how they might work the situation to their advantage somehow. Pretty words had been said by their nobles about his grand, prosperous rule and the bishop had spoken rambling, artless platitudes about Charming's piety and devotion.

Fools all of them, she thought. *Oh, how Charming would have hated it!* It all made her want to sneer in disdain. *Vile, obsequious leeches, the whole lot of them.*

No one had really known her prince but her, just as she knew that no one really knew her but him. Nobody hurt like she did now. It made her want to scream in frustration and order every one of them to leave, but she managed that much self-control at least. She played her required role of appropriately grief-stricken but stolidly enduring wife and queen all the way through the long, pretentious service. All through the pompous eulogies and insincere encomium of nobleman after nobleman, lord after lord, all through the solemn, carefully orchestrated, somber pretentiousness of vassals and knights she remained stayed and still.

Into the royal crypts, Queen Snow White swallowed her tears and withstood her grief as she followed his body, which was regally clad in his finest clothes and clutching a bouquet of small, white flowers closely to his breast. Then she stoically watched the young men set him in an empty marble coffin on a low stone dais beside cold, silent rows of his forefathers. She did not cry as they lay his sword upon his unmoving breast and retrieved his golden crown. Snow White did not wail as they passed it to her cold, numb fingers.

It was only when the young men came to seal him in the tomb that her composure collapsed. It was only when they lifted the heavy lid of the stone sarcophagus that she was overcome by panic. That was when she finally understood - Charming was leaving her. He would never return.

A million random, senseless thoughts filled her brain – illogical excuses why the ceremony must be halted, intractable reasons this tragedy could not be true, pleading prayers to the God Charming had loved so much to revisit the finality of this judgment. She knew the thoughts made no sense, but could not help herself.

Can they not see they might wake him with that racket? She thought frantically. *Surely, he will need a blanket or pillow! He will be so uncomfortable on just that rough cold stone! How will he breathe? Wait! Just a moment longer... No... This can't be right. Don't close the lid! Please... It just* can't *be right! Wait!!! Please, wait!!!*

The cover descended with a resounding crash and was then slowly pushed into place with a horrible grating and grinding of masonry, but her own tortured thoughts were even more deafening. It was only when Charming's face was no longer visible that she truly felt cut off, and just like an arm or a leg might have done upon being hewn from her living body, that severance was an agony to her.

All of the chaos of misery in her own head fought its way out in a miserable wail of grief that echoed through the stale burial chamber as the coffin sealed. Once the tears began there was no stopping them. She threw herself on the stone casket and would not be moved. No one could comfort her. It felt as though her beating heart had been cruelly ripped from her chest - like half of herself had been torn away.

Her people left her alone in her grief and the mourners slowly trickled out, but the queen remained. Hours she stayed there inconsolable, but eventually, as afternoon was turning to evening and night was coming on, two of Charming's most trusted body guards were forced to carry her physically back to the castle. They had deposited her gently in this chair in her lonely room and that was where she stayed with Charming's bouquet of stiff, dead flowers.

***

"Really," shot back the mirror incredulously, jarring her out of her miserable recollections with a tone that was something akin to anger. "I know nothing of being alone? How many decades did I hang on this dusty wall all but forgotten with nothing but pigeons and rats for company? How many years before that was I secreted away in the bed chamber of a self-obsessed mad woman?! Trust me, your Majesty, I *know* loneliness.

"In fact," continued the mirror haughtily. "I think it is you who does not understand it!"

"How dare you!" screamed the queen. "How many years did I languish as a wraith in my own castle, seen but ignored by everyone?! How many years was I friendless and hated among my own people?! How many nights did I wish fervently for death so that I might be with my parents again?! How often do I wish for that now, wandering these cold halls aimless and alone?!"

"Indeed," replied the mirror coldly. "You have known loneliness before… Think back to how you dealt with it then. What about the first time your prince left you?"

"He never did!" shot back the queen. "We spent nearly every waking moment together! Not until…"

"He did," rejoined the mirror insistently. "Maybe only for a time, but he did and you were forced to find your own strength…"

"My own…?"

"You have been no wilting blossom!" interrupted the mirror forcefully. "Why do you play the helpless spinster now? Come! Do not let your grief erase your memory. You have been strong. You have been *queen*! *See* and remember!"

Snow White did not reply. In fact she wilted. It was only with great reluctance that she raised her eyes again to the swirling vortex beneath the surface of the magical looking glass. She felt inexplicably defeated.

Have I ever been strong? She thought in despair.

It was hard to recall. When she tried, all she could think about was how sad and lonely she felt right now. How could she have ever been more than she felt in this moment?

But wait.

Was that something there? She squinted her eyes and cocked her head to the side quizzically. What was it? It bore a resemblance to flowers, but not her sad funeral bundle… What was she looking at?

"Remember, Snow White," called the mirror as its voice grew distant. "Remember what it meant to be strong…"

Chapter 10

Princess Snow White sat alone in the garden with her eyes closed contentedly. It felt as if she lounged right smack dab in the middle of an incredibly fragrant rainbow. Flowers of a hundred different varieties surrounded her and filled the air with their intoxicating perfume. Butterflies flitted here and there and birds sang among the bushes and in the treetops. It was a glorious day. The gardens were beautiful, the weather perfect, and the princess reveled in it.

Gone were her thick socks, heavy woolen skirts, and fur lined stoles, all packed away in closets and chests for yet another year. The fireplace in her chambers was cold and silent, the flue tightly closed, the windows widely open. The sun was bright and warm on her face and a gentle breeze stirred the new green leaves of the flowering shrubs around her. She had kicked off her velvet slippers and delighted in the feel of soft, new grass beneath her toes. It was lovely to finally be outside again.

Every morning for the past few weeks Snow White had gazed longingly out the window of her high tower chambers and marked the slow retreat of the snow back up the steep slopes of the tall and distant mountains. Though the spring had been long heralded by the slow return of birds and the gentle greening of bare boughs, today was the first time that being out-of-doors felt really and truly pleasurable.

There was only one thing that would have made this absolutely perfect day even more perfect in fact, and she sighed in sudden disappointment. Charming was gone this month. He had been called back to his father's country to help organize the transfer of his court to Snow White's much larger and more centrally located holdings at Castle Wolfejager. Upon his return, they would begin the arduous process of combining the two discordant sets of gentry. Charming warned her it would be a difficult process to say the least, but today those concerns were forgotten.

She missed him, of course. Her new husband could not return soon enough in her book. Though Snow White had always categorically detested winter, this year's frigid months had gone by quite quickly. As cold as it had been outside, there had been no lack of warmth in her soft, wide marriage bed. Snow White briefly recalled the feel of his strong hands on her body, his soft skin as it pressed against hers. She blushed in spite of herself. Then she smiled broadly and hugged herself at the memory. The princess would count the moments until his return, but the magnificent weather would certainly make the time go by more swiftly.

As she sat there, lost in happy thoughts about the pleasant weather and anticipation of the pleasurable attentions of her new husband when he finally came home, she looked up. She heard a group of laughing voices drawing nearer through the labyrinth of trees, hedgerows, and flowers that made up the royal gardens. A group of gaily clad and precisely painted noblewomen soon came into view as they turned the corner to Snow White's sunny nook. When they caught site of the young crowned-princess, they all curtsied appropriately.

Snow White did not know any of them very well. Though they were all technically her nobles, Lady Arglist had always kept her separate from any of the other highborn. She thought she remembered someone telling her that the woman in the lead – a pretty if rather severe looking middle-aged woman - was named Adalicia. She was the first to raise her eyes and addressed the princess.

"My!" she exclaimed with a great degree of pleasant embellishment. "We did not expect such an unlooked for pleasure, cousin! How lovely to see you here! Taking advantage of the first nice day to… unwind, I see." She paused slightly to glance at Snow White's bare feet, with apparent disapproval, but covered it quickly with the same smiling mask as before.

Snow White was still wrapped up in her own thoughts and so did not notice the uncharitable glance. Nor did she chastise the woman for addressing her as "cousin" when there was no question that Snow White was of far superior rank. She answered Adalicia pleasantly.

"Indeed, I am." Snow White smiled radiantly. "I gather you and your companions are doing the same?"

The other ladies giggled. Adalicia gave a thin lipped smile and bowed slightly.

"Quite so," she replied, still neglecting to use her princess' title. "Though, I must admit a certain envy for her ladyship." She looked at Snow White's bare feet again, barely able to keep the sneer from her lips. "I fear we are much too… self-conscious… to enjoy the out of doors as much as you. Perhaps it is because we have not spent nearly so much time in it. I understand that you are quite the woodsman! I had heard rumor, cousin, that you were raised in the forest by peasants. Perhaps that is why, her Highness, may be so much more at ease than we."

Adalicia finally used the appropriate address for her ruler. However, and Snow White was not quite sure just why, it felt like the other woman was swearing at her.

Snow White answered suspiciously. "As a small child I was, of course raised by King Garion and by my mother Queen Bemadette. After they died my care fell to the Regent, the Lady Arglist. I'm certain you are all aware of what befell after that, surely!"

"Perhaps, I've broached too tender a subject, cousin," Lady Adalicia quickly retreated. "Forgive my clumsy curiosity. I understand your... reluctance to discuss the dearly departed Regent. I apologize. Certainly, I meant no offence."

"What can I do for you?" Snow White asked shortly.

"Ah yes," Adalicia answered. "I compliment your directness, cousin. I shall get right to it then. I and the other court ladies are organizing a bit of a get together this evening to celebrate the coming of spring. We would be honored if you would deem fit to attend. Perhaps you overestimate our familiarity with your, I'm sure, most interesting exploits and travails. We have so wanted to get to know our future queen better. We would love to hear all about your... unusual adventures, and perhaps just a bit about your handsome, foreign husband? You simply must come!"

There was something in Adalicia's manner that bothered Snow White, but she could not quite put her finger on what it was. She could think of no good reason to decline. Besides, she thought, if she was going to rule this country, she should get to know those who would help her do it. The princess would not trade even a single instant she had spent with Charming since their marriage, but did suppose that she had in fact been putting off her civic duties far too long.

"I would be honored to accept Lady Adalicia's kind invitation," she replied politely. "I look forward to the chance to acquaint myself with all of you better."

"Perfect!" exclaimed the other lady, clapping her hands together in delight. "We will then eagerly await your presence in my chambers in the South Tower two hours past nightfall. Enjoy your morning, cousin."

Then without waiting to be dismissed, the courtiers retreated back the way they had come through the gardens. Snow White heard their giggling voices long after they had disappeared from view. She went back to her daydreaming, but also started to consider what she might wear to the evening's festivities. Except for an old nanny she only half remembered and the seven kind, little men with whom she had briefly dwelt in the forest, Snow White had never really had anyone that she would call a friend besides Charming. Maybe this initial awkwardness was only natural.

She adored Charming certainly, but perhaps this was her chance to finally have a few female friends as well. As she thought about it a little more, she really did begin to look forward to the evening's party. She soon collected herself and retired to her own chambers to prepare.

*

Snow White arrived promptly. Her ladies-in-waiting, all relatives of Charming himself or younger sisters and daughters of his nobles, had dressed the crowned-princess beautifully. She wore a light blue, translucent gown, and a tasteful array of fine, gold jewelry. Her face was expertly painted. Her ladies had been a bit perplexed by the idea of the future queen having to be the one to go out of her way and visit her courtiers instead of the other way around, but did not say anything. Perhaps it was just another of their mistress' foreign peculiarities.

Snow White had butterflies in her stomach as she knocked on the heavy wooden door of the apartments that Adalicia's entourage had been assigned. She waited. Then she knocked again. Several long minutes later, the portal opened to reveal a gray-haired and very proper looking serving woman. She looked Snow White up and down critically.

"Milady." The matronly women did not address the princess, but instead called back into the apartments behind her. "You guest has arrived." She turned to Snow White and gave a very perfunctory curtsy. "This way, if you please."

As the elderly servant led Snow White inside, the dull hum of conversation, the clinking of silverware against plates and glasses, and the gentle tinkle of chamber music met her ears. That all stopped as the princess came into view. She found herself in a fairly large room, well-lit by soft candle-light. A long oaken table splitting the chamber was sat all around by as many as twenty five or thirty noble women in spectacular array. At the head of the long table sat Lady Adalicia, who stood as Snow White approached. All eyes were trained upon the princess as she was led to an open chair at Adalicia's right hand.

"Ah!" cried the other lady, clapping her hands together in delight. "It is so good of you to have come! We were concerned you had changed your mind. Unfortunately, there is not much left to eat at this late hour, but I'm sure we can find you something."

Snow White furrowed her brow in confusion. "I beg your pardon, my lady, but did you not request that I arrive two hours past nightfall?"

"Oh…" Lady Adalicia looked away in mock surprise. "Is it possible that you did not receive word? I'm terribly sorry. We decided to begin just at dusk. I was sure that I sent a courier to inform those foreign women who see to you. Perhaps they failed to comprehend the message?"

Snow White's mortified face flushed intensely pink as a murmur of giggles ran through the assembly, but Adalicia barreled on.

"Still, no harm done!" she crowed with a clearly overdone degree of jocularity. "Bring our distinguished guest a glass!"

Snow White felt the calculating eyes upon her with all too vivid clarity. They seemed to undress her where she stood, judging her every flaw. Nervously, she wilted into her chair and stared down at her hands in her lap, but still she felt the weight of those unfriendly eyes.

Lady Adalicia seated herself again in her own chair and fixed Snow White with an intense expression. "So tell us about your many adventures, Snow White," she directed loudly. "Tell us of your frolics with the peasant dwarves and how you so artfully disposed of Lady Arglist, which I must say, was a masterful stroke."

"Lady Ar…?" Snow White stammered, taken off her guard.

"I mean," continued Adalicia ruthlessly. "Most young women your age and in your position would have simply waited until they were eighteen to come to power on their own, but you managed to eliminate your rival a whole two years early by winning the aid of the Geschictian Army! I must say, the burning iron shoes were a nice touch as well. It served proper warning to those who might think to oppose you."

"I…" stammered Snow White helplessly.

"Or perhaps…" Adalicia trailed off with a dangerous smile. "Perhaps that was the doing of the foreign prince? How convenient it was for him to discover our wayward princess so unexpectedly in the forest, hmm? Especially after the Regent had announced to everyone how tragically she had died – devoured in the woods by wild beasts after running away. Nothing left of her but filthy rags and a bleeding heart… But clearly she was mistaken! Because *here you are*! And then to think that on top of all of that you discovered *love* with this man?! Thank goodness for little miracles, right? It is indeed a very beautiful tale."

"I… I…" began the princess falteringly.

"Ah, look!" interrupted Adalicia yet again. "Your beverage has arrived! Please, drink up! Perhaps once your tongue has been lubricated a bit, you'll finally be able to discover your voice and illuminate us all!"

The cup set before the princess was made of coarse unpolished wood. There was a dark, viscous liquid inside and it gave off a strong, astringent smell.

"What is it?" asked Snow White uncertainly.

"What? That?" asked the lady. "I think it's called 'whiskey' – far too harsh for my taste, but I thought perhaps you would find it nostalgic. I assumed, given your peasant upbringing with those strange deformed creatures you lived with, that it would be something you were accustomed to. I obtained it from some of my servants. I believe the stable boys drink it… So,"

Adalicia pressed on giving Snow White no time to protest. "Tell us about this prince who has stolen your heart!" The noblewoman leaned forward with an intense glare. "I mean, he must be well-gifted in his loins for everyone to see so little of you since the fall. We all wondered what could have possibly befallen you, since his soldiers would not let us in to visit with our very own crowned-princess. He must have done an admirable job of keeping your attention. You have my envy."

"P'raps," chimed in a rounder, younger noblewoman to Adalicia's left dressed all in yellow but for the numerous wine stains on her bodice. She was slurring markedly and looked unsteady in her chair. "P'raps the capturing was done by our fair princess... How did you repay those foul dwarves for room and board after all? What was their price for rent? Are the appetites of little men as great as those of regular size, I wonder?"

"Indeed," giggled another. "Perhaps her experience and long practice with the peasant creatures helped her snag her new husband! I understand that a number of men like their women to know what they are doing! What say you, princess? Did you capture your prince with the skillfulness of your wandering hands or the dexterity of the muscles between your legs?"

Snow White's mouth worked, but no sound came out. Her mortified face was flushed scarlet in embarrassment. She could not summon any reply to the horrible things these women were saying.

"Now, now, ladies, please..." lilted Adalicia with a cruel smile. "Let us not be crude. *We* must consider our dignity." She fixed Snow White with a vengeful stare. "You on the other hand... I do not think you truly understand just what it is that you have involved yourself in now, girl, but I shall be most pleased to illuminate you. You are far out of your depth.

"King Garion let this kingdom fall to ruin," she went on, "just for the privilege of filling Lady Arglist's withered womb with his seed each night. If you are in fact his daughter, which I most deeply disbelieve, it still means little. You have been raised as nothing more than a common peasant and now you expect to lead people of *quality*?!"

She stood and thrust an accusing finger in Snow White's face.

"We finally rid ourselves of one usurper," Adalicia declared grandly, "who was at least of our own making, and you dare seek to saddle us with yet another - a *foreigner* who would take you to his bed for the hope of adding our magnificent country to his own backwards nation?"

"That isn't true!" shouted Snow White, at last finding her voice. "Charming would never...!"

"I will not let that happen!" Adalicia interrupted passionately, affectively drowning out the princess' protests. "My husband is the grandson of a mighty king! I have given him sons who will finally rule this country in the manner it deserves! Whatever your foreign prince might suppose, the path to the throne of Gutefehia does not lie through the gap between your legs! Now drink up, princess!"

Snow White was seized from behind. Rough hands twisted her arms painfully behind her and tilted her head back by her hair. Her mouth was suddenly filled with foul, bitter liquid. She gagged and coughed struggling to spit it out, but more of the harsh beverage was immediately there to replace it. She could not help but swallow and it burned all the way down her throat and into her belly. She immediately began to feel light headed.

"Now, let us see the princess appropriately arrayed in accordance with her station!" cried Lady Adalicia.

Though Snow White struggled to get free she could not break the grip of the hands holding her. She tried to cry out, but every time she opened her mouth, someone poured in more of those awful spirits. Someone else grasped the bodice of her fine dress and ripped it down to her waist exposing her breasts. Another unseen attacker forced a rough burlap sack, with a hole cut in the middle down around her head. All around her was derisive laughter.

"You are no princess!" cried Adalicia scornfully. "But you do play a clever game. I'll give you that much credit. A handsome prince happens upon the mythical lost princess in a lonely glen and aides her in deposing her cruel usurper! A fine story *peasant*, but I am not a great aficionado of faerie tales.

"Admit it!" she pressed. "You are a nothing but a sad pretender! A fool of a commoner who foolishly thought her pretty face alone could deceive us and better her lot in life! Admit that this foreigner forced you to claim you are the Princess Snow White! Admit that he coerced you into lying so that he might steal our country for his own!"

"It's a *lie*!" Snow White shrieked in horror. "I am Snow White! You must…" She gagged and spluttered as more bitter liquor was poured into her mouth.

Adalicia strode from behind her own chair and knelt beside the tearful and terrified princess. In her hand she held a long stave of willow wood. It was about as thick as her thumb.

"You will tell me the truth," Adalicia hissed menacingly. "Confess you are a pretender! Confess it, or I will make you suffer for your lies. *Confess!!!*"

"I am Snow White!" the princess spat intensely. "I am not a liar!"

"If you will not admit it voluntarily," Adalicia stated grimly. "I will make you tell me. You will beg to confess your every secret from the deepest, darkest reaches of your soul when I am through! Put her on the table and hold her down!" the furious noblewoman commanded.

All the air was driven from Snow White's lungs as she was drug from her chair and slammed face down onto the banquet table. She tasted blood in her mouth and felt it dripping from her nose. All around her was abusive laughter and shameful catcalling.

Lady Adalicia slowly raised the willow staff above her head and Snow White closed her eyes. She tensed in anticipation of the blow.

A loud bang echoed across the room as the door to the corridor flew open. Everyone fell silent as a tall middle-aged man with a thick grey beard strode in imperiously, flanked closely by at least two dozen soldiers. He was impressively attired all in red crushed velvet with an elaborate display of gold embroidery spider-webbing the expensive garments. Half of the soldiers wore the same color emblazoned with the golden palomino of House Gewissenhoft. The other half, were clad in the pristinely white livery of Snow White's personal guard.

The solid grey-beard took in the entire assembly of women with a hard, commanding gaze. Then his cold eyes fell on Snow White's bloodied, tear-streaked face.

"What is going on in here?" He demanded in a thick, authoritative burr. Then he quickly ordered the men to collect the unabashedly sobbing princess. "I see ye lurking there Adalicia. Step forward and explain yourself!" he commanded explosively.

"Ah, Duke Gewissenhoft," Adalicia drawled distastefully. "I did not realize that you had returned from exile."

"Apparently not!" he shouted as his men ushered the inconsolable Snow White toward the exit. "And well I did too. As soon as I heard that Arglist was no more, I knew you would waste no time slithering your oily way back in here. You play a dangerous game, my lady. You'll be lucky to keep your pretty head atop your shoulders after this. Assaulting the crowned-princess is punishable by death!"

"She is no *princess*," sneered the other lady. "She is a nobody, a peasant - the maid servant of a usurper and the whore of forest freaks and foreign princes. It is the worst sort of jest that she was ever even permitted to set foot in the royal palace! It was just fortunate that I arrived in time to amend this travesty."

"You're a fool!" countered Gewissenhoft with a reddening face and harshly pointed finger at Adalicia. He quickly swung it around to point at Snow White who was now standing miserably at his side, clutching her ruined bodice closely to her chest. "I was in attendance at this child's birth. I stood at her father's left hand at her christening! This is the princess, Snow White! She will be your queen and commands your obedience! This is blatant, naked *treason*!"

The duke turned to his sergeant-at-arms. "Lock Lady Adalicia in the dungeon and confine the rest of these ladies to this room. We'll talk to them one at a time until we figure out what exactly has happened here and what to do about it." He turned back to the crowd of Adalicia's supporters.

"This is open rebellion against the crown!" The duke declared sternly. "Any one of you who keeps your head will be lucky! If you'd like any chance of it at all, you'd best tell the truth and beg for mercy!"

As his men escorted Lady Adalicia out of the room she shrieked, "My husband will hear of this outrage! When he sits upon the throne I will see your head set atop the castle gates to be food for crows and flies, Gewissenhoft! We will never bow before the doxy of a foreign usurper!!!"

"Get her out of here!" he growled. "You men manage this lot!" He directed the majority of his soldiers. "You three, help me escort the princess back to her own chambers."

Chapter 11

When Snow White arrived back at her own rooms, her ladies-in-waiting nearly had a conniption. They were positively scandalized when they saw her pallid, bloodied face and learned of her ill-treatment. They vowed passionately to report the outrage to her husband, who would then surely set things to rights!

Snow White knew that they meant it. Moreover, she knew they would *do* it, but truly wished they would not. She honestly would rather Charming never find out about it at all.

She felt like a stupid, brainless dupe - thoroughly ashamed of herself and humiliated by her own foolish naiveté. Not since Arglist had spitefully overseen her noxious upbringing had the princess felt so thoroughly detested and abused. It all made her feel achingly alone.

Though all she really wanted to do was to hide in her bed beneath the covers and cry until Charming came home, Duke Gewissenhoft was not swift to leave. He waited impatiently as Snow White's retainers saw to the disposal of their lady's ruined clothing. They quickly attired her in something appropriate to receive her liege man and sat her in a fine wooden chair in her study. The duke knelt and bowed respectfully before her, but all the miserable princess could do was stare at her hands folded in her lap as if expecting a scolding.

"Your Highness," the duke began gruffly. "Are you alright? Those women didna' hurt you, did they?"

Snow White shook her head, but did not look up.

"Well that is good," Gewissenhoft sighed, but then looked up pointedly. "Now, I do na' wish to sound rude, Your Highness, and I do beg your pardon, but princess, if I may, what on Earth were you thinking going off with Lady Adalicia by yourself into her chambers, filled with her supporters and accompanied by no guard at all?! Her husband and your father *detested* each other!"

"I... I..." Snow White began meekly. Then she sobbed and put her face in her hands. "I'm such a fool! I just wanted to make some friends!" She cried. "I just wanted them to *like* me! I didn't really know any of them, but I thought they are supposed to serve my father's throne, and I knew they hated Arglist as much as anyone and... and... I don't understand! Why don't they like me? Why do they *hate* me?!"

Duke Gewissenhoft sighed. Then he stood and stepped over to awkwardly pat his young ruler's shoulder.

"I am sorry, lass," he apologized gently. "I should have known that you would na' know a thing about the ways of the court. After all it was I who protested most loudly when the Regent was sequestering you away from it. Nearly half your life it was... I even got banished for my trouble! I should have come back sooner, but the snows made it impossible, and I..." He stopped and narrowed his eyes thoughtfully. Then he hesitantly asked, "Do you... Do you remember me, Snow White?"

Snow White turned her red-rimmed eyes up to look at the large, older man. She thought he seemed familiar, but could not really be sure. Then she recalled the device on his soldiers' livery. Her eyes opened wide and she flung her arms around the neck of the astonished duke.

"Uncle *Horsey*?" She asked in disbelief. "I can't believe... But Lady Arglist told me that you were dead! Oh, I've missed you!" Then she could seem to find no more words, but sobbed into the older man's shoulder.

Snow White had vivid memories of riding on Uncle Horsey's shoulders to grab apples off of the trees in the garden and sitting on Uncle Horsey's lap to hear his wonderful stories. She had always loved the pretty horse on his shirt, and for a child of five or six, Gewissenhoft was far too difficult to say.

The Duke smiled slightly.

"Aye lass," he murmured fondly. "It's Uncle Horsey." He sighed in relief then smiled broadly. "I knew it was you! You have your mother's look. Ah, I'm so glad to see you grew into such a fine, pretty thing. Now," he went on hesitantly. "I know you've had a bad night, lass, but I really must speak with you about your courtiers... about the danger you're in"

"What do you mean, Uncle?" asked Snow White guilelessly.

"Well," he began. "I think tonight should give you some indication, but please understand that Arglist's claws are still drawing blood. After your father died, she methodically began to get rid of those who had been closest to him. They either met with unfortunate 'accidents' or, like me, were simply sent away. Her greatest fear was that you would come of age and replace her. Those who were allowed to stay at court were either your father's enemies, or simple toadies, yes-men, or other hangers on. Chiefest among those was Duke Finsterkeit. I believe you know his wife?"

"Lady Adalicia," murmured Snow White, the blood draining from her face.

"Aye," replied the Duke. "He is your father's first cousin and was something to happen to you, he would be next in line to the throne of Gutefehia."

"So," stammered Snow White with saucer-wide eyes. "They were trying to *kill* me?"

"I don't think so." The Duke shook his head. "Like she said, I don't believe that Lady Adalicia really believes you to be King Garion's daughter. Had she believed your claim, she might have tried to poison you, or smother you in your sleep, or hire someone else to do you in, but she would have never attempted that public fiasco this evening. It's treason and demands her head.

"None of us have really seen you for years, Arglist kept you so isolated. I think Adalicia sought to convince everyone that you were just a pretender – a puppet set up by an ambitious foreign prince. Had she tried to kill you and failed, that would have only added legitimacy to your claim in the minds of many. I'm sure she thought it in her best interest to prove you were no threat and that she held no fear of you. By publically humiliating you then driving you out of the castle, I think she hoped to demonstrate that you had no real power or standing. Then with you discredited and no other claimants to the throne, her husband, Duke Finsterkeit, could have walked right in and started planning his coronation!

"I think I may have changed that now," the duke added. "I would like to think that my word still lends you legitimacy, but there will still be at least some who will question. They know I, like your father, could not abide Finsterkeit, but…" he met her eyes and smiled. "I have fifteen hundred good men inside these walls presently and they do not! Also, I have word from many of your father's old allies. With you back on the throne, they are returning to the court. Once they get here, I do not believe that even Finsterkeit will have the support to openly question your claim to the throne. Until then however, things… well… They're tricky. Even after we have more of your supporters around, that will not make you safe. I need you to be wary, Snow White. Trust no one!"

"No one except you?" Snow White asked with a small scowl. The whole time her uncle talked, a sinking feeling along with that horrible whiskey in her stomach, was making her feel decidedly ill.

Gewissenhoft laughed out loud. "That's *just* what I mean. Good lass. Just like that, trust no one… Not even me! Trust yourself."

"And Charming," Snow White added stubbornly.

"Ah yes," replied the duke, taking a seat on a nearby chair. "Forgive me for sitting, Majesty, these old legs get tired easily these days… I'd forgot about that. You're a married woman now!"

Snow White smiled and nodded shyly.

"Is he a good man, Snow White?" the duke asked seriously. "Will he be a good king?"

"He is the best man I have ever known, Uncle," she replied sincerely.

"Well," he answered. "I hope that's true, your Highness." He held up a hand to forestall her protest. "I'm not saying I don't believe you, lass. It's just that he will have to truly be a special kind of man to see you through to the end of this mess. Are you happy?"

"The happiest I've ever been in my whole life, Uncle," she said, and it was the truth.

Gewissenhoft smiled again. "I'm happy for you then, but I do want you to understand something. None of this is going to be easy. If it was just a question of confirming your claim to the throne, it would be difficult. We will still also have to decide on a Regent to rule in your stead until you turn eighteen.

"Trust me." He shot her a knowing look. "Finsterkeit will want it to be him, and that lass, would be very bad for your health. Now, in addition to all of that, we must also convince the other nobles that a foreigner sitting beside you in your father's throne is a good idea! Gutefehia and Geschictia have not been to war in a couple of generations, but neither have we ever been best friends and allies. Even the nobles who support you will be worried that a handsome face with pretty words is taking advantage of you to steal your kingdom. I must say, I'll be the happiest man in the world if all you say about this Charming fellow is true, but I'm a bit worried about that myself. I understand that things happened quickly and what's done is done, but it would have been better to consult with your nobles before getting married."

"I trust my husband down to my very soul, Uncle," Snow White stated emphatically. "He will not betray me."

Duke Gewissenhoft nodded and sighed in resignation. "Very well, princess. If you can knit our two peoples together, your country will emerge all the stronger for it. The lands your children inherit will know no rival, but that, your highness, is a very, very big 'if'. Still, I will do my best to see it done." He got up to leave.

"Uncle," Snow White asked hesitantly. Everything the duke told her was still bouncing around inside her head like so many glass marbles scattered across a hard, stone floor. It left her feeling out of sorts and helpless. How could her life have changed so drastically since just the morning?

"Yes, your Highness?"

"What will you do with Lady Adalicia?"

"What will *I* do?" he asked with a chuckle. "The question, lass, is what will *you* do?"

"Me?" Snow White asked in shock. "Why me? Like you said, I'm not old enough to rule yet!"

"No," Gewissenhoft responded. "But you were the wronged party. Also, you must send a clear message to Finsterkeit that he will not simply be able to waltz in and sweep you aside. I think if you pronounce punishment on his wife, it will definitely help your standing among the nobles. I promise you this; my men will have put the fear of God in those women upstairs by now. They were party to treason. You asked me why they hate you? Well the short answer is most of them don't, but they sure as Hell don't want to find themselves on the wrong side of a contested succession. If they believe Finsterkeit and Adalicia to have the upper hand they'll take their side. If they feel you are more likely to prevail, they'll want to be the best friends you ever had… at least to your face."

"But that… that's awful!" the princess stammered. "Don't they have any values? Any loyalties? Don't they believe in anything?!"

"Dear Princess," sighed the old man. "You are young and you have a good, loving heart. You always did. I'm glad to see that Arglist was na' able to take that from you, but you know better than anyone what wickedness might abide in the hearts of people. The nobles are scared. They are afraid of change. Arglist was an evil shrew, but the nobles knew what to expect from her. They know what to expect from Duke Finsterkeit and Duchess Adalicia. You on the other hand, are a very large question mark. They have no idea what kind of future you'll make for them or what their position in it will be. Values? Beliefs? They value their own status. They believe in power. That is what you must show them if you are to rule."

"You said," she breathed weakly. Snow White was suddenly afraid that she might throw up. All the blood drained from her face. "You said that Adalicia's treason would cost her head… You… You expect me to do that?"

Gewissenhoft really did laugh at that. Snow White was mortified by his reaction, but the duke swiftly apologized. "I'm sorry, Your Highness. That was unkind. No. I do na' expect you to swing the axe yourself! As much I would like to see the Dear Duchess a good ten inches shorter, I would council against it."

"But you told her…"

"I know, princess," he responded quickly. "I did. I just wanted to let her sweat over it a bit in the dungeon for a while – let her think that I might make a rash, emotional decision, but that would be a disaster. It would push Finsterkeit too far. It might even lead to a full-blown civil war! At the same time however, you cannot appear weak. Lady Adalicia and any others who helped her to humiliate you must be punished or you will surely lose every shred of credibility that you possess with the court."

Snow White swallowed. She did not want to punish anyone. She just wished the whole sordid mess had never happened, but she had to admit that what Duke Gewissenhoft said made sense.

"What do you think I should do, Uncle?" Snow White asked in a near whisper.

"If it were me," began the Duke carefully. "I would stop short of killing her, but make sure her humiliation matched your own. It must be harsh enough that none of the other nobles will even think of trying something similar. A public strapping perhaps? Fifty strokes or more, I should think. Then banishment. The nobles must fear you, princess."

"Thank you, Uncle." Snow White nodded slowly. She still did not like the sound of it at all. "I shall conduct court tomorrow morning. There I shall have Lady Adalicia brought before me and I… I will render my decision."

"Very well, princess," the duke rose and made to leave. "If you will excuse me, Your Highness. I think I shall find my own bed. I've put some men at your door so you need fear no reprisal this evening. I took the liberty of setting up in the quarters your father always kept for me. I trust that meets with your approval."

"Of course, Uncle," Snow White replied. "And thank you for saving me. I am indebted to you."

"You are the crowned-princess of Gutefehia, Snow White," he replied with a small, pleased smile. "I did my duty, nothing more. It breaks my heart what you had to go through tonight, lass, but please, do take a lesson from it. You can never let your guard down."

He left.

Snow White's ladies-in-waiting got her ready for bed. They turned down the covers, tucked her in, and put out the candles. Snow White lay down, but did not sleep. How could she? The great four poster bed felt too big and lonely without Charming. Again, she found herself fervently wishing that her brave husband would suddenly reappear and save her from the mess in which she now found herself.

She dreaded the morning. Whatever was she to do with Lady Adalicia? Thoughts of seeing the other woman beaten, no matter how shabbily the duchess had treated her, made Snow White feel sick again.

She must have agonized over what to do for hours, but ultimately Snow White was struck by a thought. She was not going to be king. Having a malefactor beaten was something her father would do, but what about her mother?

She still remembered her a little. Snow White recalled that she had been beautiful, kind, and fair. There had even been a life-sized portrait of Queen Bemadette stuffed into a closet in a disused bedroom where it had evidently been forgotten and remained unknown to Arglist. Snow White had discovered it shortly after her father died and used to spend hours just sitting, staring, and fantasizing about how life would have been different if her mother had not grown ill. What would her mother do?

If her father had been gone and Queen Bemadette had been forced to deal with such unpleasantness, what would she choose? As the gentle moonlight on the floor slowly made its way from one side of the room to the other, Snow White pondered what the answer to that question might be.

*

The next morning, per her orders, Snow White was roused early by her ladies in waiting. Then she had them ransack all of the storage rooms where her parents' old things were stored. It proved a worthwhile endeavor. In a dusty old chest, but carefully packet in oiled parchment with pungent herbs to keep the moths away, they made a spectacular find.

Her ladies dressed her regally in a long, black velvet dress, tooled all over in silver. It had once belonged to the queen, Snow White recalled, and had been one of her mother's favorites. It was the dress from the portrait, in fact.

She set her mother's crown, liberated from Lady Arglist's chambers, upon her own brow and looked at herself in her tall vanity mirror. She smiled at what she beheld. Snow White had not been formally crowned, but if she was going to make a statement, she decided, she would *really* make a statement.

She allowed her women to fix her hair in the style she remembered her mother often wore – tightly braided and pinned in an attractive bun at the crown of her head. They also painted her face and served her breakfast, but Snow White could not even think of eating. Her stomach was twisting and turning into knots as she made her way slowly to the throne room flanked on either side by two rows of six guards each clad in livery of the purest white.

As she entered the throne room she noted that every last noble currently residing in Castle Wolfejager had already crammed into the audience chamber. A full platoon of Gewissenhoft' s men lined up shoulder to shoulder all around the outer edge of the great hall and the old duke himself stood dutifully at the base of the dais on which sat the thrones of the king and the queen. As Snow White crossed the cavernous room, all conversation ceased.

When she ascended the dais and turned to face the assembly, there was a collective gasp. The mouths of all of the older courtiers fell open and their eyes gaped in amazement. What they saw seemed impossible. It was as if they had just witnessed a ghost wander into their midst. Even the duke was taken aback.

Snow White swept her gaze over the thunderstruck nobility in a way she hoped was imperious. Her dark eyes were cold as she addressed them.

"My Lords and Ladies," she began sternly, her voice echoing through the large chamber. "I am saddened that I must first address you all under such unfortunate circumstances, but evening last, an act so egregious was committed that I cannot overlook it. It pains me to report an act of high treason against the very throne of Gutefehia. Despite being but mere months removed from the overthrow of a vile usurper, it appears that there was at least one other rebellious malcontent who failed to take a lesson from that pretender's fate. Bring in the accused!"

It took only a few moments for her command to be obeyed. Snow White caught sight of Duchess Adalicia's maddeningly contemptuous face as she, along with four other women, were led into the throne room. Each was flanked on either side by a guard in Snow White's spotless white livery. Adalicia wore an insolent expression of smug arrogance as she entered, but when she caught sight of Snow White standing regally atop the dais her mouth fell open and she nearly fell to the floor in her surprise.

"Q... Queen Bemadette?" she stuttered. "But that is im..."

"Silence," hissed the princess. She did not raise her voice, but no one had any trouble hearing her. "Duke Gewissenhoft, please read the list of charges against these women."

"Yes your Highness." He took a step forward. "Duchess Adalicia of Finsterkeit, you stand accused of libelous slander against the crown. Furthermore you stand accused of assault seeking to inflict bodily injury upon the very person of the crowned-princess. Finally, you stand accused of high treason against the throne. What say you to these charges?"

The duchess was clearly taken aback. It was apparent, just as Duke Gewissenhoft had explained to the princess the night before, that she fully expected Snow White to be proven a fake. Even among those who laughed loudest during the previous evening's abuses and humiliations, there was no denying whose daughter Snow White was now. It seemed almost as if the long dead queen had returned from the grave to render judgment on her daughter's behalf.

Adalicia's mouth worked, but no sound came out.

"Many of you have heard of the indignities I was forced to endure at the hands of the pretender, Arglist," Snow White began stonily. "I was dressed in rags, forced to sleep on the cold stone floor, beaten, berated, forced to complete menial labors, but *never* in my life have I been forced to endure humiliation of the like I experienced last night."

The room was dead silent. Every noble in attendance stood pale and uncertain, no one daring to breathe as they waited for the princess to pronounce her doom.

"Perhaps you were not here when the Lady Arglist met her fate, Duchess," she went on coolly. "It was my husband's wedding present to me. Do you recall it?"

Adalicia's eyes grew wide. It was obvious that in her mind's eye she could see the iron shoes heating in the forge already. The other accused courtiers likewise gasped or cried out. One of the ladies, (the fat one who had worn the yellow dress the night before), toppled over backwards in a dead faint.

The gruesome manner Charming had chosen to punish her tormentor had actually disturbed the young princess deeply, but she felt no compunction at all in invoking the veiled threat now. Her head understood what her uncle told her the night before, but in truth she had agonized over the prospect of bloody revenge. It was just simply not in her nature to be vindictive, but she understood how important it was for her to appear strong before the court.

Snow White knew that she must act a queen. She wanted Charming to be proud of her when he finally returned.

Her deliberations had been agonizing, but very early in the wee hours of the morning, she had come to her decision. Now she took a deep swallow as she prepared to deliver it. She directed her icy gaze to the duchess and her cronies.

"Your treasonous acts demand death!" she declared dramatically, and another of Adalicia's coconspirators, one of the women who had forced that vile whiskey down her throat, joined her fat friend on the floor. The remaining women threw themselves prostrate before the throne.

"Mercy! Highness!" They all cried together. "Please! Mercy! *Mercy*!"

Adalicia screamed the loudest.

"However," Snow White continued coldly, ignoring their pleas. "It took weeks to get Arglist's nasty burnt stench out of the castle and taking your heads would leave a ghastly mess all over my floor. I could hang you all, I suppose." She continued with mock thoughtfulness. "But all that would do is attract rats and crows to gnaw at your fetid remains, and I certainly do not want any more vermin in Castle Wolfejager." She glared at Adalicia pointedly. "So I find myself in a quandary. Your deeds warrant death, but I have decided that I am unwilling to allow you persons to cause me any further inconvenience at all!"

The three prostrate women raised their heads uncertainly, daring to hope but unsure of what the crowned-princess could possible mean.

"You have all already afflicted me with infinitely more worry and care than I feel like I am willing to put up with," the princess continued. "Therefore, I have decided that it is you who shall decide your fate."

The room remained as silent as a tomb. All of the assembled nobles looked at each other askance - not at all sure they understood the princess' decree.

"Right here, right now, before all of the court," Snow White continued at length. "You shall render appropriate punishment on each other, but be warned," she cautioned dangerously. "If I am not satisfied, flaming dance shoes shall be the least of your concerns... I am waiting!"

There was a brief pause where nothing and nobody stirred. However, and not surprisingly to Snow White, Adalicia reacted first. Desperate with the idea that she might have been offered a way to wriggle out of her predicament, she leapt to her feet and immediately pulled the dress of the lady on her right over her head. Then she proceeded to kick and punch the screaming woman until she had managed to rip the whole thing off, leaving the other lady naked and bruised before the entire court.

Then the woman on Adalicia's left, well put out that the duchess had dragged her into this mess in the first place, quickly afforded her similar treatment, grabbing the neck of her dress and ripping the bodice down to her waist, barring her breasts. The two women who had fainted shook their heads groggily and sat up, making them ready targets for the ladies already engaged in the melee.

Very shortly the frightened, angry women were wrestling around in the floor in various states of undress. They kicked and clawed, bit and slapped, ripped out hair, screamed, squawked and otherwise made a horrible racket. It did not take the other nobles in attendance long at all to see the humor in all of this and they quickly contributed to the cacophony with hoots of laughter, catcalls, and even thrown garbage. It was clear that the well-born of Gutefehia were enjoying the unexpected entertainment immensely.

Snow White was not amused. She did not find it funny at all. She found the whole display - both that of her abusers as they tried to save their own wretched skins as well as the reaction of the other nobles - to be utterly disgraceful. They were like a pack of wild dogs, so quick to turn on each other! She realized in that moment she could trust none of these people. Had her Uncle not unexpectedly appeared the previous evening, it very well could have been her wallowing down there in the floor, covered in blood and filth.

She let the spectacle go on, but quit watching it. Time seemed to move excruciatingly slow, but eventually, the five convicted tired themselves out so much they could barely move. They lay panting in the floor even as the rest of the court continued to laugh and scream.

"Enough," said the crowned-princess at last.

The room immediately fell silent.

"On your knees."

The exhausted ladies struggled wearily to comply. They looked awful. Two of them were completely naked and had prevalent scratch marks, bite marks, and bruises all over their bodies. Adalicia had prominent, bloody claw marks crisscrossing her bare chest and face and looked to be missing a couple of teeth as well. All of them had bloody patches of missing hair on their heads and were covered in the garbage thrown by their peers. They meekly planted their noses in the floor.

"We are satisfied," declared Snow White simply. "Now get out of my castle."

The women struggled awkwardly to comply. As soon as they rose and rushed their staggering way toward the exit, the room exploded again. More vile language and humiliating taunts were thrown in addition to more refuse, and even more scandalous substances. Snow White shook her head, utterly appalled.

"Court is adjourned!" She declared, and then abruptly left the room.

Duke Gewissenhoft caught up to her quickly in the hallway.

"That, my princess," he declared with an enormous grin. "That was pure *brilliance*! You could not have possibly planned it any better! Now no one can accuse you of being heavy handed and all will be properly disabused of the prospect of treating you lightly. Very, *very* well played, Highness!"

Snow White stopped and turned her face toward her uncle. Her eyes were already red-rimmed. Tears flowed freely down her soft cheeks.

"I hate those people, Uncle!" She cried bitterly. "I hate them all! They call themselves 'highborn'." She sniffed derisively. "They're *animals*! Every one of them! Beastly, hateful animals!"

Gewissenhoft's smile faded and he put a sympathetic hand on Snow White's delicate shoulder. He gently brushed away a single angry tear on her cheek.

"I canna' say ye nay, Highness," he confessed gently. "They're a bunch of badly behaved, spoilt children, but that is why, my princess, that they need a wise and just ruler like you who will na' lead them astray, nor indulge their baser urges."

"I can't stand them, Uncle," the princess shook her head stubbornly. "I will rule them if I must... as I am God-bound to do, but I do not like them. I will *never* trust any of them near me again! Not a single one!"

"That, My Dear," replied the duke soberly "is very wise."

Chapter 12

"But that just illustrates my point!" insisted Snow White, when she came back to herself. "Without Charming, I was set upon like a doe among wolves. I was helpless! Foolish! Useless! You are right in that I am constantly surrounded by people, but they are no friends of mine. They have no love for me even as I assuredly have no love for them! They are leeches and vipers who I am duty-bound to oversee!"

"All of them?" asked the mirror.

"All of them," stated Snow White bitterly.

"But it was not Charming who came to your rescue." The mirror pointed out calmly.

"That's different!" cried the queen. "Duke Gewissenhoft was sworn to my father! He said himself that he was only doing his duty!"

"Come now," prodded the mirror incredulously. "Do you really believe that?"

Snow White did not reply. She looked down at her feet. She felt the tears coming again.

"No," she dejectedly said at last, "but don't you see?" She suddenly felt her oh-so-familiar moribund despair coming over her again. It seemed almost like a thick dark cloak thrown over her heart and soul. "All of the misery in my life, all of the pain, all of it has been caused by being so often forsaken! I've spent more of my life alone than not! My mother left me little more than a baby. Then my father left me with a demon to oversee my upbringing! Now my husband has abandoned me to loneliness and despair. If you are so wise Mirror, then tell me! Why does everyone good in my life leave me? Why does everyone I love abandon me and go away?! Why did Charming leave me all alone again?! Why? *Why*?!"

"Why did you try to leave him?"

"I never…" the queen began, but almost immediately, she paled and trailed off. Snow White felt a sinking feeling in the pit of her stomach. She knew of what the mirror spoke. It took her again.

***

"I really don't understand what you are so worried about, Darling," Charming was still trying to be patient, but Snow White could tell that he was beginning to get annoyed by her persistence. "People talk and foolish, stupid people tend to talk loudest and longest, but that's all it is – insipid, meaningless blather!"

"Charming, this is serious!" the princess insisted. "I know as well as anybody that there has been grumbling among the nobles for years, but this is different! I have it on the best authority that Duke Neid rode away to a private audience with your father this morning and last night I overheard Lady Verleum talking with Lady Stolz in the gardens. They said that the duke is putting pressure on your father to make you put me aside! They say I am barren and will not give you an heir! Your nobles hate me! You know full well that they have never liked the idea of the merger of our two courts. Ever since we first were wed they have resisted it at every twist and turn. If Duke Neid now stands with them, they will see this as a perfect opportunity to stop it once and for all. They will demand that you divorce me!"

"Nonsense!" the Prince shouted, practically leaping from the throne in his agitation. His voice echoed harshly through the large, empty audience chamber. Snow White reflexively recoiled with a horrified look on her face. Charming had never shouted at her before.

This was not the first time they had had this discussion, but this was the first time Charming had reacted so passionately. Before, he had always dismissed her concerns with an unconcerned laugh or a gentle kiss and changed the subject. The prince seemed surprised at himself. He took a deep breath, looked down at his toes, and then ran a slow, heavy hand through his short, blond hair. Tenderly he took Snow White's hand and pulled her into a firm embrace. He forced himself to smile and kissed her forehead. He began stroking her long black hair. The prince sighed deeply before speaking.

"Dearest Piece of My Heart," he began gently. "You know that malicious gossip, petty political posturing, betrayal and intrigue are just the price we pay for our nobility. There will always be awful people around us saying hurtful things, but remember that you are a queen! I am a crowned-prince! They do not rule over us, but we over them. The hateful yowling of a couple of jealous courtiers of no consequence or influence means *nothing*! Fear not, My Dearest One. Do not doubt my love for you. I would never…"

"It is not your love I doubt, My Husband!" Snow White interrupted in frustration. "It is your father's patience! Duke Neid is your father's chief minister! He is not just some malcontent young knight or baron! His muster is equal to that of your father and his holdings second only to those of the crown! He knows better than anyone that you must have an heir! If he has turned against me…"

"We do not know that to be true," Charming interjected, taking her firmly by the shoulders and forcing her to meet his eyes. "All of that is speculation based on the half-heard gossip of two fools. Like you said, Duke Neid is my father's chief minister. His responsibilities are vast. They might be meeting about anything! King Justice adores you! My mother loves you. I love you! They would never…"

"Your father must love his kingdom first," Snow White shot back bitterly. "As must you when it is your turn to be king! The line must be continued. You might not like it, but you must have an heir and you know it!

"Your father will have you set me aside," she murmured forlornly, wringing her delicate hands. The longer she talked the more certain it seemed. "Then he will select another bride for you, but do not grieve. He will find you one who is young and beautiful, who will give you twenty sons…"

"Enough!" roared Charming. "I swear to you! IT WILL NOT HAPPEN!!!" I would abdicate my throne before I let that occur! I have cousins! I have uncles! Let them…"

"Uncles like Prince Arger?" Snow White countered incredulously. "Can you imagine what damage that man would cause if he ever became king? He is next in line and…"

"The person who is next in line does not always survive to become king…" the prince muttered cryptically.

Snow White shook her head in frustration. Why did he insist on being so stubborn?

"So are we then to trust to fate that he will be run over by a cart? Or thrown into the river by his horse? Or contract some deadly disease? Or…" her voice grew quiet and grave. "Or do *you* mean to do him harm, Husband? Who else would you slay before choosing an acceptable replacement for yourself?"

Charming did not reply.

"I am sorry, my love," the princess apologized. "As much as I love you, as much as I want us to be happy together, I will not permit you to murder for me... There is just no way around it. You must have a child and I cannot give it to you!"

Charming took her chin in his hands. He forced her to look into his eyes, willing that Snow White should see the sincerity and determination inscribed upon his very soul.

"No one will take you from me, my princess," he pronounced intensely. "*No one*! If the problem is a lack of a child, then I will give you one now – right this very moment!" He pulled her tightly against him. "I will put my baby in your belly upon this very throne and then no one will be able to say you ill ever again!"

Snow White had been doing her best to maintain her composure, but the passion of Charming's will – a determination and love that should have reassured her, instead made her want to scream. She was acutely aware of his hands on her, his body so close to hers. The raw, animal power of his anger kindled a purgatory of desire. She felt her body responding to his and wailed in despair.

"My womb is dead!" she cried. "My insides are as barren and dry as the desert. I have as much chance of conceiving as a corpse! Do not torment me! I have failed you as a wife! I have failed you as a princess! I have even failed my own people as queen! I... It's just no good, Charming! We just have to accept..."

"I WILL NOT PUT YOU ASIDE!!!" Charming thundered. "On my honor and by the wounds of the very God in Heaven, and upon His gleaming, golden crown, and upon Heaven and Earth and everything that abides in between the two, I swear it to you! Lands, riches, power... It all is *meaningless* without you. My marriage vows to you were not just some pretty speech that I wrote for a lark. They were not some mummers play to be performed for pretension and vainglory at our wedding. They were a sacred oath on my soul before the very throne of God! Nothing short of death will ever part us. I swore so before and I reaffirm it now! No one will *ever* take you away from me Snow White. NO ONE! Believe that. Trust in me. I will never put you aside."

Snow White suppressed a sob. After the first spasm of her grief passed her lips, she knew, she would not be able to contain it. Charming tried to pull her close again, but she just could not bear his touch at the moment.

She pushed away from him and ran out of the chamber. He did not follow her and that was telling. There was no question that her dear, sweet husband adored her. He did not want what she said to be true, but that was not the same as believing she was wrong.

Snow White had begun the discussion with her husband afraid that he might be persuaded by the king and the other high ranking nobles to put her aside, but she suddenly realized it was even worse than that. She knew now that he would never admit the impossibility of their situation. Just as he had said, he would never give her up, even if that meant destroying himself and his kingdom. She could not let him do that. Snow White loved him too dearly, but what was she to do?

She fled to her chambers, unceremoniously evicted her ladies-in-waiting, and barred the door behind her.

Why does it have to be this way? She lamented to herself. *Why am I so relentlessly afflicted? What am I to do? Oh God, what do I do?!*

If Charming defied his father and did not divorce her, in the absence of an heir, Prince Arger was certain to assert his claim to the throne. If he were to do that, more than half of the nobles would protest and the other half would join him. They might even rebel! Then Snow White's Gutefehian nobles were sure to be pulled into bloody conflict as well. Even if it did not come to that, they would put even greater pressure on Charming to divorce her and that pressure would be relentless. At the very least, they would insist he take a concubine.

Snow White knew more than a few young noblewomen who would be willing to take on that role. There were more than a few even now who all but threw themselves in the path at Charming's feet when he passed. The Prince had been married to his foreign queen over a decade with still no children to show for it and it did not take any great feat of mental acuity to divine why. Already, impervious to the Gutefehian Queen's affront, pliant young women were circling her husband like sharks who had scented the first drops of blood in the water.

Who would it be? Snow White thought miserably. *Lady Blasa, perhaps?* She was a fire-headed, large bosomed beauty from the north who made no secret of the fact that she would be perfectly willing to visit Charming's bed.

Maybe Lady Eadaion? She was only sixteen, flaxen haired, and willow thin. She was widely regarded as an exquisite beauty and her father, Baron Adalrik, would sell his very soul for some royal influence, let alone his daughter.

Please, please, please let it not be Lady Ysuelt! She was dark haired and gorgeous but there was never any light behind her pale eyes when she smiled. She was cold and calculating and reminded Snow White forcefully of Arglist.

The queen threw herself miserably onto the bed in a weeping heap and closed her eyes tightly. She tried to banish their faces from her thoughts, but in her mind she could see each of the other women in turn, naked in her bed, sweating, moaning, writhing - triumphantly riding *her* husband like a stallion that they had just captured and tamed.

Snow White could not bear it. She screamed in fury and frustration and leapt from her bed. She swept a great pile of books and a heavy crystal flower vase from the top of her breakfast table. They flew across the room to land with a resonating crash against the Cistercian tiles. The vase shattered into a million pieces sending the fresh, white roses within skittering across the floor.

Snow White stood staring at the mess she had made and felt a little ashamed of herself. It was not in her nature to throw tantrums. She took a deep, calming breath, knelt slowly and began to dejectedly gather the squashed flowers and broken glass onto a nearby silver tray.

She gasped. The broken crystal was incredibly sharp. The queen watched in fascination as blood welled from a small cut on her index finger and began to drip down her hand onto the floor.

No. She was letting her imagination run away with her. Charming would never leave her. He would never take another. He had sworn that he would cleave to her unto death and Snow White knew the man well enough after so many years that she believed him. That was just the problem – his high-minded devotion to her would ruin him.

There was just no escaping it. However long and hard she thought about it, she kept coming back to the same inescapable conclusion - Charming needed an heir and she could not give him one. He would refuse to let her go, and destroy himself in the process.

She was being selfish. He had saved her so many times. Now it was her turn to rescue him, whether he wanted her to or not. Snow

White could not think of herself now. She must think only of her beautiful husband.

Snow White stared at the blood dripping from her hand, so starkly red against her alabaster skin… Through her hopelessness the beginnings of a plan started to take shape. It was a desperate plan and the idea of it frightened her to her core, but she knew that it would work. It must work! Fate had dealt her a cruel hand, but there was no use in crying about it anymore. She had one last card left to play and now was the time to play it.

Snow White wrapped a handkerchief around her injured finger. Then she walked purposefully to her wardrobe and riffled about within. Eventually she found a quill, ink, and parchment. She sat down at her drawing table and began to write:

My Dearest Charming,

> *For most of my life I have been as a fallen leaf - tossed hither and thither by a bitter gale, going wherever that the fates willed. Often, it has blown me into danger and strife, fear and pain. Whatever other tricks the fates may have played upon me however, I bless the rare, warm breeze that brought me to you.*
>
> *The last eleven years I have spent with you have been the happiest of my life. I never thought to know love so complete as that which you have shown me. I know now more about love than I ever dared dream even existed before! You taught me that, and I shall be ever grateful.*
>
> *I cherish the time I have been allowed with you, but realize now that what we have enjoyed cannot last. How could something so perfect actually exist in the waking world? It has all been a dream, a faerie tale – one that I believed in whole heartedly from the core of my being for ages and ages! But like all great stories, ours too must now come to an end. The burdens of our positions are too great for even the boundless strength of our love to lift.*
>
> *You deserve a woman who will meet your every need, but I have fallen short. Your line must continue. Your kingdom must have an heir and though it rends my heart to admit it, I cannot give that to you. Though you swear to me that you will keep me forever regardless of this damning*

truth, and it lifts my heart to know the depths of your devotion to me, I cannot allow it. You would abandon your responsibilities and destroy yourself on my behalf. I love you too much to ever let that happen. Were I to indulge such a selfish longing, it would devastate both of our countries. Therefore it falls to me.

I will not leave you, for I have not the strength. I will not flee from you, where I know you would only follow. There is but one place where I might go and release you completely. There is only one where you will not be able to pursue me.

Please know, what I do now, I do out of the greatest love and undying devotion to you, My Darling. My only regret and greatest sorrow is in how I have failed you. Grieve but a little while only. Then, I pray you, please choose another bride who is worthy of you. Believe that I truly wish you every happiness to come.

With undying love and limitless grief that our dream must end,
Your Own,
Snow White

Snow White laid the pen down and stared at the words on the paper. Her narrow shoulders shook and her tears slapped audibly against the dry parchment in the otherwise silent room. With a shuddering sob she opened her desk drawer and drew forth a long, thin knife that she used for opening letters. She stared at the glittering blade and took a deep swallow. She hesitated.

Once she did this there would be no going back. She turned her problem over in her head one last time but still arrived at the same damning conclusion; without a baby, she was useless. Charming must have a child. She had to release him. There was no other way.

She drew the blade quickly across her right wrist then her left. It only hurt a little bit and that surprised her. The queen had imagined an act of such finality would have had a rather more dramatic finish – weeping and wailing, writhing on the floor... But no. There was only a mild throbbing from her damaged wrists and a steady drip, drip, drip of crimson. She watched in morbid fascination as bright red blood ran in runnels across her pale, white skin and began to pool on the desk in front of her before dripping onto the floor.

Snow White swallowed, more than a little shocked at what she had done, but ruthlessly banished any lingering regret. What was done was done. All there was left to do now was wait.

She had hoped this noble gesture would make her feel better. She had hoped to find peace in her decision by putting her own feelings aside and saving her poor prince from himself, but she did not. She still felt miserable. Snow White still longed for her husband.

The queen crossed her arms in front of her and laid her head down on the writing desk, sobbing at the unfairness of it all.

Oh Charming! She thought. *How I will miss you!* She felt very sleepy all of a sudden.

"Oh, my poor husband," she whispered softly as she drifted into darkness. "Why must it be this way? I am so, so sorry…"

Chapter 13

Snow White did not know how long it had been, but the first thing she became aware of was a very loud noise. Soon it came again, then again, then repeated in rapid succession. The noise crescendoed into a cacophony of crashing, splintering wood and disembodied voices. She wondered who could be so inconsiderate while she was trying to rest.

The weary princess groggily tried to protest the disturbance, but found she could make no sound. She realized she was lying on her back in the floor. She tried to sit up, but could not make herself move. Why was she so weak? Snow White could not make out who, but someone seized her arms. Slowly the unintelligible murmur of garbled voices solidified into words.

"…Press it tightly lass, tightly!" One of the voices began to make sense. "Hold on as if it was for dear life! We've got to get that bleeding stopped!"

Who is that? Thought Snow White sleepily.

"Hold on there, Snowy," the voice commanded urgently. "Don't you give up on me now. Don't you dare! You've got to fight!"

Is that Erfreut? She thought muzzily. *What is he doing here?*

"Oh, my God! What did you do?!" demanded a different fear-stricken voice. Suddenly she was yanked up from the floor. Someone was shaking her "What did you do?! Please, Snow White, stay with me! Wake up! Wake up! Snow White! Can you hear me? Snow White!!!"

With what felt like the most laborious effort, Snow White forced her eyes open. Her face felt stiff and sticky, caked with congealing blood. At first, the lights and sounds all melded together in one incomprehensible blur, but gradually the shapes started to make sense.

First, she saw Anja, her youngest lady-in-waiting holding her left wrist in a white knuckled grip, a tattered strip of fabric that looked like it had been hastily torn from the woman's own dress clenched in her fingers. The strip, her hands and her clothing were all stained with blood. A frantic, equally sanguineous Erfreut did the same to her right. They both looked nearly hysterical.

It was then that she recognized she was still in her drawing room. At first she thought the door to the corridor was open, but instead she realized it was simply gone. The hinges hung wildly askew from broken brackets on the wall and large splintered chunks of lumber littered the floor around her. A heavy, military-styled axe lay in one corner as if hastily tossed.

Then over her shoulder, she saw who it was who grasped her. Charming held her against his chest in a grip that was nearly painful, it was so tight. His breath was hot and labored at her ear. It was hard to focus, but when she caught sight of his eyes, she could not help but be appalled.

His cheeks were streaked with blood. His eyes were wild, terrified, but also desolate. The misery and fear she saw reflected therein was soul crushing. In her whole life, she had never seen her husband look so lost. It made her want to cry, but she just did not have the energy.

Oh God, she thought in horror as she felt the darkness dragging her down again. *I have done this to him.*

"Please don't leave me, Snow White," he begged shamelessly. "By God, Erfreut, she's so pale! She's going cold! Please come back, Snow White! Please come back…"

*

There were dreams then – long and strange and dark. Snow White thought it felt like drowning – as if she struggled to keep from being pulled down by something large, faceless, and sinister, but then again it was different. They were not dreams like she was used to. Not even her old childhood nightmares about Arglist and losing her parents, not even her delirium after being poisoned filled her with the same degree fear and dread. These were poignant beyond expression, but at the same time confusingly lacking of substance.

Later, Snow White would only recall that they had shaken her to her very core and terrified her beyond words, but she could not ever express adequately exactly why. Perhaps there were some mysteries too secret to share even with herself, she would muse later, but there was no denying their transformative power. Much to her own surprise and disbelieving joy, the visions ended. She woke again to the living world, but she was not the same.

Snow White opened her eyes slowly. Something in the doing felt strange and new, like she was, in fact, doing it for the very first time. She felt easily just as weak as before, and the gentle light hurt her eyes, but she noted that she was no longer lying in the floor. She was tucked carefully into her own bed and dressed in her own frilly night gown.

Her wrists throbbed painfully and she looked down with a grimace. She saw that they were heavily wrapped with clean white bandages. The equally pristine light of morning streamed through an open window, dramatically illuminating a slouching figure at her bedside. Sitting on a simple wooden stool was Charming. He looked awful.

Her husband was slumped forward, apparently having dozed off, but his face was haggard and worn. He had still not changed out of the bloody shirt from before and Snow White could clearly see more dried, black blood cementing patches of his otherwise light, blond hair. She could not help but clench her eyes tightly closed again and weep. By God, what had she been thinking?

It was a tiny sound, but Charming started awake anyway. When he perceived that his wife was conscious he knelt beside the bed and crushed her to his chest. Then the prince started sobbing in earnest as he rocked her back and forth, stroking her long black hair. In all their years together, it was the first time that Snow White had ever seen him cry, and she did not know immediately how to react. It made her feel miserable.

Charming took her face in both hands and kissed her firmly on the lips, then he crushed her head against his chest again.

"Thank God," he murmured affectedly. Then he just kept repeating. "Thank God, thank God, thank God..." all the while squeezing her so hard that Snow White wondered the two of them did not simply fuse together.

After no short time he met her gaze with furious eyes.

"What were you doing?!" He demanded abruptly. "What on Earth did you think you were doing?! Do you know how badly you scared me?! Do you know what losing you would have *done* to me?! Do you know..."

He found he couldn't continue, so he crushed her body against his again and kept crying into her soft, black hair. They stayed that way for a very long time this time, but eventually

Charming regained enough of his composure to ask a single poignant question.

"*Why*?!" he breathed strickenly.

Snow White simply deflated. The pain and confusion she saw scrawled so clearly across her husband's face was devastating. She felt guilty, but still miserable and hopeless. She found she could not meet his eyes.

"I don't know what to do, Charming!" she wailed in a voice that was breathy and weak. The Prince had to strain to hear her. "I just don't know what to do! It's killing me! I want your baby, Charming! I want it so badly! I want to give that to you so much! You deserve that from me and I... I... I... What do I *do*, Charming?! I don't know what to do..."

Charming released her and let her lie back in the soft bed. Then his head fell to her chest. He clenched his eyes tightly closed. For a long while he simply delighted in the scent of her. Gratefully, he listened to the gentle rhythm of her heartbeat.

"Just be with me," he murmured at last. "That is all I ask from you. Promise to share this life with me. Strife may come. Worry may come. Disappointment and grief may come, but I promise you this - We shall always weather those storms better together than we ever will apart. There is no knowing what tomorrow holds for us, my queen. There is no knowing the count of the days we have left together. Do not try to shorten them. Let us share in them, whatever might come, as long as we may."

"I'm sorry, Charming," she cried. "I'm *so* sorry. I wasn't trying to hurt you. I was trying to help! To fix everything and make things simpler! I want to help you! I... I..."

She trailed off but was struck by an unbidden thought. It was something she had pondered before, something that she had dreaded honestly, but for some reason, this time it did not seem quite so bad.

"*I* could help you find a concubine," she suggested sincerely "I would be *oh* so careful about it, Charming! I know what you like – maybe better than anyone! I would be sure to choose someone who would be young and pretty and good to you..."

She perked suddenly. "Oh! Lady Rillia is sweet. She is a small dainty thing, but very, very pretty. I only know her a little bit. She strikes me as the shy type, but she seems nice. We might even grow to be friends! I could learn to live with it, Charming. I really could! And I promise I will love your baby like it is my very own. I will. I…" He silenced her with a kiss.

"I am the one who is sorry," he sighed. "It rends my heart to see you so hopeless and sad. This was eating at you far more than I let myself realize. I should have put a stop to all the gossip a long time ago. I never want you to doubt your place in my life, Snow White. That is immutable… I would not know how to live this life without you."

He put both of his hands on her shoulders and met her gaze with every bit of the sincerity and devotion in his heart shining seriously in his piercing blue eyes.

"And one other thing I want you to understand very, very clearly." He leaned even closer. Snow White had never seen him so intense. "You are my wife. I will never take any other woman into my bed. I love, you Snow White. I love you so very much. I cannot be without you. My life is worthless without you to fill it! Promise me quickly now. I must have your word! Promise that you'll *never* try to hurt yourself like this again. Promise you'll never try to leave me. Swear it!"

Snow White met his eyes. The depth of the love as well as the pain she saw both overwhelmed and shamed her. Ultimately, she nodded and Charming gathered his wife to him. He held her firmly against his broad chest for a very long time.

"Charming?" Snow White ventured at last. "Before… before in the audience chamber, you… you said… you said that you would put your baby inside me…"

"I said that, my love," he sighed. "I swear I did not mean to make you feel…"

"Do it now," she interrupted.

"Snow White!" He exclaimed. "You nearly died! You can barely move! I don't think…"

"No," the princess insisted, weakly shaking her head. "I… I need you. Please, Charming. I feel so empty. I need to be filled with you again, right now. Do this for me. Do what you said. Please, try one more time. Do it now."

He shook his head helplessly. "Snow White, I…"

"Please?" she pressed again.

Charming looked at her gravely. Then he sighed. He nodded slowly and kissed her. The prince carefully pulled down the concealing sheets and gently lifted her night dress above her waist. She was still ghostly pale and very, very weak.

Charming knelt on the bed and pulled down the waist band of his blood encrusted trousers. He placed his hands on her knees with but a featherweight of touch and gingerly spread them apart. When he finally entered her, she sighed.

It was not long or elaborate. The prince was careful and slow, scared to death that he might accidentally injure his ailing wife in her infirm state, but it was just what Snow White needed. She did not know why exactly, but suddenly she felt safe again. Soon, he tensed and Snow White felt his release pulsing inside of her. She smiled and closed her eyes.

The prince readjusted her nightgown delicately. Then he lay down beside her and covered them both with thick blankets. He pulled her tightly against his body and held her like he would never let her go. They both slipped quietly into sleep.

Though she could not be absolutely sure, Snow White liked to think that this day was the day it happened. Later, she would turn it over in her head until she was certain that this gentle but sincere moment of hesitant love making was the one that finally brought about the miracle. A little over a fortnight later, well after she was up and about again, the princess became afflicted by regular bouts of nervous stomach that kept her abed until late in the morning. A week after that, it was with great joy and fanfare that the royal household announced that the queen was indeed with child.

Chapter 14

Snow White stared down at the silvery scars on her wrists shame-facedly.

"Why did you do that, Snow White?" the mirror murmured. "Why did you try to go away?"

The queen shook her head. "I was a fool. I was a fool to despair. I learned my lesson though. After… After that… my relationship with Charming was even better! After that it was perfect. I learned a hard lesson, but maybe I needed to."

"What was the lesson?" asked the mirror softly.

Snow White was silent for a long moment. It felt like a sleepy sort of awareness was waking up in her brain, like a great juggernaut of understanding was slowly rousing itself into motion.

"That it is foolish to despair," she whispered, "that there is always hope."

"Are you sure that you've learnt it?" asked the mirror again. "Are you sure that is what you really believe?"

Snow White said nothing, but continued to stare down at her hands.

"Will you look, but once more Snow White," the mirror asked softly. "Will you look one, last time?"

Snow white nodded and raised her eyes. There in the mirror was a small bundle of tiny white flowers. They were all dead, petals dropping from dry stems like a miniature shower of snow flakes, and Snow White sobbed at the sight of them. Again she experienced the now familiar plummeting sensation, but barely noticed. All of her attention was fixed on that sad, withered bouquet.

***

How long had she stared at the bundle of the flowers lying across her legs? It must have been ages and ages certainly. If she closed her eyes, she could perfectly reconstruct ever petal, every shriveled leaf, every twist and fold of the knotted black ribbons binding them together. There was nothing especially remarkable about the flowers really. They were of a variety that could be found on nearly any hillside all throughout her kingdom, but for some reason, she simply could not tear her eyes away.

There was a knock at her chamber door, but the queen made no move to answer. All she could do was continue staring at the poor withered bouquet on her lap. A few moments passed and the knock came again.

Snow White clenched her eyes tightly shut.

Go away, she thought miserably.

But the knocker did not go away. The heavy oaken door creaked open. Snow White heard soft footfalls on the plush carpet and the swishing of fabric as someone nervously made their hesitant way across the room. When the unknown visitor reached the queen, the noise stopped. Silence stretched between the two for a long moment.

"Mother?" Came a hesitant young voice. "Lady Anja told me that you've been sitting here all day. Won't you come and eat something, Mother?"

Snow White still made no reply. She just continued fixedly starring at the sad white flowers.

"It's so very cold in here, Mother," her daughter tried again. "Shall I have your maid build you a fire?"

Snow White put her face in her hands and wept. She did not know even really why she was crying. Raven had said nothing that should have upset her, but inexplicably, she again felt devastated. Princess Raven came around her mother's chair and knelt in front of the queen. She looked up into Snow White's sorrowful face, forcing the queen to see her.

"Please Mother," Raven pleaded. "You must eat! It has been three days since we got back from Geschictia. You shall make yourself ill!"

The queen moved finally, cupping a thin, weak hand on Raven's cheek. Her daughter was so pretty and so sweet. Charming had prized her beyond anything else that he possessed. She had been a joy to him in his old age and Snow White had given that to him. She almost smiled at the thought

"Please, Mother," Raven begged again. Piercing blue eyes met Snow White's intensely. "Please, come with me. Come and take some dinner. You'll feel *worlds* better! And… and I can have a minstrel come and play for just you and me! Wouldn't that be nice, Mother? Wouldn't that make you feel better? Come with me. Please?" Those huge azure eyes watched her expectantly.

Oh God, those eyes!

So clear and kind… Like calm mountain pools they were. Gazing into hers so deeply, so sincerely, just like…

Snow White's shoulders began to shake. A fat tear fell sparkling down to decorate the dry petals like a shimmering diamond. A wail of despair that sounded as if it had been ripped from her very soul echoed through the silent chamber and then many more soon followed. Raven wrapped her arms around her mother and the queen buried her face in her daughter's hair.

Those eyes, those eyes, she thought miserably. *Please don't look at me with those eyes!*

"Please mother," Raven's own voice was beginning to quiver. "Please, come back with me."

Snow White knew that her daughter's concern should make her feel better. She knew it should, but it did not. It honestly felt confining.

What do I care anyway? The queen thought.

What was there to tie her to this miserable, disappointing world any longer? What had it ever given her but pain, and pain and more pain? All she had ever valued in it was Charming and now… All she felt was empty… Empty and abandoned and alone, *so* alone!

She wanted fiercely to leave it all behind. She wanted to be with her husband, but she had promised him. Snow White had sworn to him even, never to try and take that path again.

"Mother, *please!*" Raven begged, tears beginning to tremble unsteadily in her own voice. The young princess could see her breath and was starting to shiver in the dark, frigid bed chamber. "It's so cold in here… You mustn't stay. It's not good for you. You'll get sick!"

Snow White could only continue weeping in response.

In desperation, Raven shook her.

"Please, Mother!" the princess pleaded. "Look at me! Come with me to my room! It's warm in there! We can eat together! It's not good for you to be so alone! Please stay with me! *Stay* with me, Mother. Don't leave me alone with this! Don't push me away! Stay with me! Please, stay with me…"

Raven was sobbing. "Will you not look at me, Mother? Will you not even *look* at me?! Why don't you see me? I'm right here beside you! Look at me! Please, don't leave me! LOOK AT ME!"

The tears just would not stop. All Snow White could do was shake her head. She did not look up. Why could everyone just not simply leave her be? Why could they all not just go away and leave her alone? Why must even her own daughter torture her – tormenting her with those beautiful, terrible, taunting blue eyes?

Raven covered her pretty face with her hands and rushed from the room. Snow White continued weeping and weeping until she was certain that she surely must have no tears left. Then she sat still again, staring at the dead bouquet.

The queen never did go to dinner.

***

"There is always hope," the mirror softly murmured as the queen came back to herself. "Didn't you see it? Perhaps you did not know it for what it was then, but do you not see it now?"

"Oh Raven," sighed Snow White tearfully.

She raised her head slowly and met her husband's piercing azure gaze in the mirror's shining surface. The image shifted and changed until it was her daughter that she saw within. Raven's face was so like her own, so like his. The desperate and despairing words the girl had spoken cut to the queen's heart. They were too near what she had said herself, alone in her bed, deep in the night to her dead husband when no one was around to hear. The sense of loss tearing at Raven's soul was too much like her own.

The princess grieved for her mother as one already dead and it broke the queen's heart to realize it, but she was not surprised by the revelation - not really. The truth had been right before her eyes the whole time. She had been wallowing in grief for over a year now. In that time she had barely looked at her daughter. It was selfish she knew, but she had avoided even her, because every time she looked at the girl Charming's eyes looked back.

"I'm sorry Raven," Snow White whispered to the ghostly image in the looking glass. "So sorry..."

The image shifted once more. Charming gazed down at his wife sadly.

"You cannot follow me, Snow White, yet you try and try and try," he murmured softly. "And you have left our princess alone..."

"What my love?" Snow White felt the tears rising to her eyes and into her throat as she spoke.

She knew it was just the mirror now. She knew it was nothing more than an illusion – ghosts of her own memories and secret thoughts, but it sounded *so* like him! Even this brief glimpse of Charming struck straight to her core. "I don't understand."

"I did not abandon you, my heart. I did not wish to leave you." He began as tenderly as he had always treated his beloved wife and queen. He chided her, but his voice was gentle and patient. "Neither your father nor your mother wished to leave you either, but it was not our choice to make. The time appointed to every man is his own, but you would make my end yours as well. I want to remain a piece of your heart, but I did not wish this.

"You cling to the ghost of my memory and have forgotten to live, my dear, dear Snow White," he went on. "Where I have gone you cannot follow, not yet... But please, I beg of you to live for me in the intervening time. We will be together again. Do not doubt it. It is as sure a thing as my love for you and yours for me ever was... But neither should you hasten it! Do not leave Raven alone as I have had to leave you.

"I had no choice when I was called away from you, but you abandon our daughter by choice... I must go. You must stay, but I beseech you to look around. You are not nearly as alone as you think... I am sorry for this pain I have caused you. I wish you to be happy again... I love you..." He began to fade.

"Wait Charming!" She cried desperately, again pressing her hands and face against the cool reflective surface. "Please don't leave me again! I cannot bear it again! Come back to me! Come back to me! Come back..."

The queen collapsed into an inelegant heap weeping every bit as bitterly as the day her husband had died. It felt like her heart was breaking again. Despite his words, she still felt abandoned and alone.

"He lives on in her, you know." The mirror ventured softly. "And so he shall in her children as well. For that matter, so shall you! He is not really gone if you but look for him, in her and in yourself, but you know all of this. Remember, I merely show what already exists within you. It is nothing more than a reflection. In your heart you know my words to be true, because if you examine them you will discover what they are in fact... They are your own."

"What should I do mirror?" asked Snow White tearfully on her hands and knees in the filthy floor.

She hardly looked a queen at all. Her beautiful green dress was sullied black in places from dust and bird droppings. Her make-up was streaked all across her face from weeping, and the delicate circlet on her brow was wildly askew. Her soft hair stood out in every direction.

"I feel so much pain... I still feel so empty... I think I know what to do, but it is so hard. I don't know if I can..."

"I am a mirror," it replied flatly. "I do not offer advice. I simply show that which is right in front of me. You must decide how to act on what you see. You can run from it or you can embrace it. I think you can guess what your stepmother decided..."

Queen Snow White nodded and quieted her tears. She took a deep steadying breath and wiped her red-rimmed eyes. In that moment something seemed to click. She suddenly felt a new resolve that had not been there before. She straightened and quieted her tears.

"Mirror," she murmured at last. "I am sure. The lesson was learned… just forgotten, just… muddled and buried, but I remember it now… Thank you." Then she stood regally and smoothed the front of her filthy dress. Without another word she turned and walked from the room.

Snow White strode straight down the steps and on out into the hallway beyond. The queen did not skulk this time, but strode confidently. Even though those she met along the way looked askance at their ruler's disheveled condition, she did not hide from them, but greeted each warmly, whether maid or noble.

The queen made her way back to the throne room and seated herself, not on her own throne, but upon that of her king. In short order, most likely at word of her unusual behavior and outlandish appearance, Erfreut swiftly appeared and bowed low before her on creaking, knobby knees. He looked Snow White up and down curiously before speaking.

"Is everything well, my queen?" he hesitantly asked in his artificially cordial voice.

"You recommended a diversion earlier today, my steward," stated the queen regarding her diminutive minister evenly.

"I did, my queen," he answered uncertainly.

"Tell me then," she asked as robustly as she had said anything in a great long while. "Of those favored by Princess Raven, which of the court minstrels are unengaged this evening?"

"I believe that Minstrel Heiter is free," the elderly dwarf replied thoughtfully. "Lady Raven often requests him for her parties and such..."

"Then please inform Minstrel Heiter that I request his presence in my chambers at dinner this evening and that of my daughter as well if she is otherwise unengaged..." She paused, but then smiled broadly. It was the first time she had made the gesture in a very long while and certainly the first time that she felt genuinely mirthful in the doing. "We have wedding plans to discuss."

Erfreut answered his queen's smile with a positively silly grin of his own. His courtly manners fell from him like an avalanche.

"There's my Snowy!" he declared happily. "Welcome back."

Snow White laughed merrily and her longtime friend laughed right along with her. After a moment, Erfreut regarded his queen seriously.

"If you don't mind my askin', my queen..." he ventured carefully, "and I'm certainly not complaining, but... What happened?"

Snow White gave the little man a tiny smile.

"I took a good long look in the mirror, my friend," she sighed. "Charming and I had a wonderful life together. I shudder to think what all of these years might have been like without him, or even if I would have had them at all!"

Erfreut nodded sagely.

"I would not give back even an instant with him," the queen went on. "But I do him no favors by clinging to his ghost for all the time I might have left to me. He loved me Erfreut. He loved me so very deeply! He would not want me to go on mourning him forever." She looked down shame facedly. "In fact," she murmured. "He would be ashamed of me now."

"Your Highness!" exclaimed the aged dwarf. "He never would! I..."

Snow White held up her hand and gifted her old friend a small self-depreciating smile.

"You're a good friend Erfreut, but a terrible liar. Yes, he would." She took a purposeful breath. "I've been neglecting Raven shamefully. I've been terribly selfish and have not helped her to plan what should be the happiest day of her life..."

"There is still a great deal of planning left to do, my queen." The old steward noted kindly. He offered another gentle grin as he stepped upon the raised dais and took his queen's hands once more in his own. "And Raven will be glad to have her mother back... I understand she is a bit... Nervous."

"I know, Erfreut." Snow White nodded seriously. "I pretended that I did not for a long time because I could not..." She stopped and amended herself. "Because I *did* not want to admit it, but I know. My daughter and I have much to talk about. A wedding can be stressful, even a bit frightening... To say nothing of the honeymoon!"

They both laughed, but as Erfreut turned to carry out his instructions Snow White called him back.

"Oh! One more thing... When you plan dinner this evening have Chef prepare whatever it is Raven likes best, I'm sure he knows."

"I'm sure he does, Majesty." He smiled up at her once more. "Of course, I will see to the details, Highness... but if I might say so... and at the risk of sounding impudent..."

"You are welcome to be impudent whenever you wish, my old friend," laughed the queen in genuine amusement at the wizened dwarf.

"Well then, I'll say it... I'll be sure and see to everything for tonight... And I think it's about damned time too!" the old dwarf chided before bowing his way out of the room.

Snow White laughed at the frank little man as he went. Then she called for her sorely neglected ladies-in-waiting to help her get cleaned up for her upcoming, festive evening.

That night, mother and daughter enjoyed an extremely entertaining affair, the first for both of them since the King had died. The sumptuous dinner was followed by music, and music by a very candid discussion about weddings, marriage, and even just a touch about motherhood. Snow White enjoyed the exchange. It reminded her of her own marriage to Charming so long ago.

Raven was honestly and truly scandalized about what would be expected of her on her wedding night. Mother assured daughter however, that it was actually quite enjoyable and something to look forward to rather than to fear. Her daughter's naiveté on the subject was as endearing as it was horrifying to the queen when she thought about how near she had come to leaving the girl so ignorant about matters of love.

She still saw Charming in Raven's eyes. Snow White still felt the pain of her husband's passing, but it was a bittersweet pain now. She began to find the faintest glimmer of hope that perhaps in fact she could really be happy again.

Two weeks later Princess Raven married Prince Edel before the entire kingdom. A wizened and bent Duke Gewissenhoft snored softly on the front row of pews next to Lady Anja who seemed quite overwhelmed by the unexpected honor. The queen gave her daughter away with Erfreut at her side, looking on proudly. Together the two old friends smiled on the newlywed couple with sincere joy.

As Prince Edel and Princess Raven said their "I do's", a soaring hawk cried loud and shrill, far overhead. It was as if in blessing of the young couple. Much feasting and dancing and revelry ensued, and the queen was as merry as anyone there.

The years passed and Raven and Edel had many children to begin filling the empty space in the old queen's heart. Although she still missed her king dearly, she rediscovered the joy in her life. Even after dear Erfreut passed on, she filled the empty hole that he left with the happy memories she had shared with him and the new ones she was making with her family.

Snow White never again climbed the narrow stair to Arglist's tower, but she did see to its yearly cleaning and the eviction of the resident pigeons. The mirror stayed right where it had ever been, but the queen had no desire to look into its depths.

This was not because she feared what she would see however, but rather because she already knew. The magic mirror, like any other, only showed that which was right in front of it. Snow White felt she saw that quite clearly now. Her own vanity table glass was sufficient to the task. As she stared into its very ordinary depths each morning, she still divined important truths about herself.

She saw a noble queen ruling her small kingdoms prosperously and at peace with her neighbors. She saw a dutiful mother finally available to her daughter - even befriending her woman to woman rather than simply mother to child. She saw an aging grandmother surrounded by little ones who adored her. She saw a sad little princess who had finally released the bitterness and pain of the past. She saw a lonely young girl who was lonely no longer. But most importantly, she saw a princess of raven hair and skin of purest snow with lips like the red, red rose who had finally found her happily ever after.

And so she remained to the end of her days, until at last she and her king were reunited once more.

The End

www.ingramcontent.com/pod-product-compliance
Lightning Source LLC
Chambersburg PA
CBHW030541130626
46552CB00006B/2357